The Open Door, And The Portrait

Mrs. Oliphant

The Open Door, and The Portrait

The present edition is a reproduction of previous publication of this classic work. Minor typographical errors may have been corrected without note; however, for an authentic reading experience the spelling, punctuation, and capitalization have been retained from the original text.

ISBN: 978-1-63637-437-6

CONTENTS

I

THE OPEN DOOR 1

II

THE PORTRAIT 58

I

THE OPEN DOOR

I took the house of Brentwood on my return from India in 18—, for the temporary accommodation of my family, until I could find a permanent home for them. It had many advantages which made it peculiarly appropriate. It was within reach of Edinburgh; and my boy Roland, whose education had been considerably neglected, could go in and out to school; which was thought to be better for him than either leaving home altogether or staying there always with a tutor. The first of these expedients would have seemed preferable to me; the second commended itself to his mother. The doctor, like a judicious man, took the midway between. "Put him on his pony, and let him ride into the High School every morning; it will do him all the good in the world," Dr. Simson said; "and when it is bad weather, there is the train." His mother accepted this solution of the difficulty more easily than I could have hoped; and our pale-faced boy, who had never known anything more invigorating than Simla, began to encounter the brisk breezes of the North in the subdued severity of the month of May. Before the time of the vacation in July we had the satisfaction of seeing him begin to acquire something of the brown and ruddy complexion of his schoolfellows. The English system did not commend itself to Scotland in these days. There was no little Eton at Fettes; nor do I think, if there had been, that a genteel exotic of that class would have tempted either my wife or me. The lad was doubly precious to us, being the only one left us of many; and he was fragile in body, we believed, and deeply sensitive in mind. To keep him at home, and yet to send him to school,—to combine the advantages of the two systems,—seemed to be everything that could be desired. The two girls also found at Brentwood everything they wanted. They were near enough to Edinburgh to have masters and lessons as many as they required for completing that never-ending education which the young people seem to require nowadays. Their mother married me when she was younger than Agatha; and I should like to see them improve upon their mother! I myself was then no more than twenty-five,—an age at which I see the young fellows now groping about them, with no notion what they are going to do with their lives. However; I suppose every generation has a conceit of itself which elevates it, in its own opinion, above that which comes after it.

Brentwood stands on that fine and wealthy slope of country—one of the richest in Scotland—which lies between the Pentland Hills and the Firth. In clear weather you could see the blue gleam—like a bent bow, embracing the wealthy fields and scattered houses—of the great estuary on one side of you, and on the other the blue heights, not gigantic like those we had been used to, but just high enough for all the glories of the atmosphere, the play of clouds, and sweet reflections, which give to a hilly country an interest and a charm which nothing else can emulate. Edinburgh—with its two lesser heights, the Castle and the Calton Hill, its spires and towers piercing through the smoke, and Arthur's Seat lying crouched behind, like a guardian no longer very needful, taking his repose beside the well-beloved charge, which is now, so to speak, able to take care of itself without him—lay at our right hand. From the lawn and drawing-room windows we could see all these varieties of landscape. The color was sometimes a little chilly, but sometimes, also, as animated and full of vicissitude as a drama. I was never tired of it. Its color and freshness revived the eyes which had grown weary of arid plains and blazing skies. It was always cheery, and fresh, and full of repose.

The village of Brentwood lay almost under the house, on the other side of the deep little ravine, down which a stream—which ought to have been a lovely, wild, and frolicsome little river—flowed between its rocks and trees. The river, like so many in that district, had, however, in its earlier life been sacrificed to trade, and was grimy with paper-making. But this did not affect our pleasure in it so much as I have known it to affect other streams. Perhaps our water was more rapid; perhaps less clogged with dirt and refuse. Our side of the dell was charmingly accidenté, and clothed with fine trees, through which various paths wound down to the river-side and to the village bridge which crossed the stream. The village lay in the hollow, and climbed, with very prosaic houses, the other side. Village architecture does not flourish in Scotland. The blue slates and the gray stone are sworn foes to the picturesque; and though I do not, for my own part, dislike the interior of an old-fashioned hewed and galleried church, with its little family settlements on all sides, the square box outside, with its bit of a spire like a handle to lift it by, is not an improvement to the landscape. Still a cluster of houses on differing elevations, with scraps of garden coming in between, a hedgerow with clothes laid out to dry, the opening of a street with its rural sociability, the women at their doors, the slow wagon lumbering along, gives a centre to the landscape. It was cheerful to look at, and convenient in a hundred ways. Within ourselves we had walks in plenty, the glen being always beautiful in all its phases, whether the woods were green in the spring or ruddy in the autumn. In the park which surrounded the house were the ruins of the former mansion of Brentwood,—a much smaller and less important house than the solid Georgian edifice which we inhabited. The ruins were picturesque, however, and gave importance to the place. Even we, who were but temporary tenants, felt a vague pride in them, as if they somehow reflected a certain consequence upon ourselves. The old building had the remains of a tower,—an indistinguishable mass of mason-work, overgrown with ivy; and the shells of walls attached to this were half filled up with soil. I had never examined it closely, I am ashamed to say. There was a large room, or what had been a large room, with the lower part of the windows still existing, on the principal floor, and underneath other windows, which were perfect, though half filled up with fallen soil, and waving with a wild growth of brambles and chance growths of all kinds. This was the oldest part of all. At a little distance were some very commonplace and disjointed fragments of building, one of them suggesting a certain pathos by its very commonness and the complete wreck which it showed. This was the end of a low gable, a bit of gray wall, all incrusted with lichens, in which was a common door-way. Probably it had been a servants' entrance, a backdoor, or opening into what are called "the offices" in Scotland. No offices remained to be entered,—pantry and kitchen had all been swept out of being; but there stood the door-way open and vacant, free to all the winds, to the rabbits, and every wild creature. It struck my eye, the first time I went to Brentwood, like a melancholy comment upon a life that was over. A door that led to nothing,—closed once, perhaps, with anxious care, bolted and guarded, now void of any meaning. It impressed me, I remember, from the first; so perhaps it may be said that my mind was prepared to attach to it an importance which nothing justified.

The summer was a very happy period of repose for us all. The warmth of Indian suns was still in our veins. It seemed to us that we could never have enough of the greenness, the dewiness, the freshness of the northern landscape. Even its mists were pleasant to us, taking all the fever out of us, and pouring in vigor and refreshment. In autumn we followed the fashion of the time, and went away for change which we did not in the least require. It was when the family had settled down for the winter, when the days were short and dark, and the rigorous reign of frost upon us, that the incidents occurred which alone could justify me in intruding upon the world my private affairs. These incidents were, however, of so curious a character, that I hope my inevitable references to my own family and pressing personal interests will meet with a general pardon.

I was absent in London when these events began. In London an old Indian plunges back into the interests with which all his previous life has been associated, and meets old friends at every step. I had been circulating among some half-dozen of these,—enjoying the return to my former life in shadow, though I had been so thankful in substance to throw it aside,—and had missed some of my home letters, what with going down from Friday to Monday to old Benbow's place in the country, and stopping on the way back to dine and sleep at Sellar's and to take a look into Cross's stables, which occupied another day. It is never safe to miss one's letters. In this transitory life, as the Prayer-book says, how can one ever be certain what is going to happen? All was well at home. I knew exactly (I thought) what they would have to say to me: "The weather has been so fine, that Roland has not once gone by train, and he enjoys the ride beyond anything." "Dear papa, be sure that you don't forget anything, but bring us so-and-so, and so-and-so,"—a list as long as my arm. Dear girls and dearer mother! I would not for the world have forgotten their commissions, or lost their little letters, for all the Benbows and Crosses in the world.

But I was confident in my home-comfort and peacefulness. When I got back to my club, however, three or four letters were lying for one, upon some of which I noticed the "immediate," "urgent," which old-fashioned people and anxious people still believe will influence the post-office and quicken the speed of the mails. I was about to open one of these, when the club porter brought me two telegrams, one of which, he said, had arrived the night before. I opened, as was to be expected, the last first, and this was what I read: "Why don't you come or answer? For God's sake, come. He is much worse." This was a thunderbolt to fall upon a man's head who had one only son, and he the light of his eyes! The other telegram, which I opened with hands trembling so much that I lost time by my haste, was to much the same purport: "No better; doctor afraid of brain-fever. Calls for you day and night. Let nothing detain you." The first thing I did was to look up the time-tables to see if there was any way of getting off sooner than by the night-train, though I knew well enough there was not; and then I read the letters, which furnished, alas! too clearly, all the details. They told me that the boy had been pale for some time, with a scared look. His mother had noticed it before I left home, but would not say anything to alarm me. This look had increased day by day: and soon it was observed that Roland came home at a wild gallop through the park, his pony panting and in foam, himself "as white as a sheet," but with the perspiration streaming from his forehead. For a long time he had resisted all questioning, but at length had developed such strange changes of mood, showing a reluctance to go to school, a desire to be fetched in the carriage at night,—which was a ridiculous piece of luxury,—an unwillingness to go out into the grounds, and nervous start at every sound, that his mother had insisted upon an explanation. When the boy—our boy Roland, who had never known what fear was—began to talk to her of voices he had heard in the park, and shadows that had appeared to him among the ruins, my wife promptly put him to bed and sent for Dr. Simson, which, of course, was the only thing to do.

I hurried off that evening, as may be supposed, with an anxious heart. How I got through the hours before the starting of the train, I cannot tell. We must all be thankful for the quickness of the railway when in anxiety; but to have thrown myself into a post-chaise as soon as horses could be put to, would have been a relief. I got to Edinburgh very early in the blackness of the winter morning, and scarcely dared look the man in the face, at whom I gasped, "What news?" My wife had sent the brougham for me, which I concluded, before the man spoke, was a bad sign. His answer was that stereotyped answer which leaves the imagination so wildly free,—"Just the same." Just the same! What might that mean? The horses seemed to me to creep along the long dark country road. As we dashed through the park, I thought I heard some one moaning among the trees, and clenched my fist at him (whoever he might be) with fury. Why had the fool of a woman at the gate allowed any one to come in to disturb the quiet of the place? If I had not been in such hot haste to get home, I think I should have stopped the carriage and got out to see what tramp it was that had made an entrance, and chosen my grounds, of all places in the world,—when my boy was ill!—to grumble and groan in. But I had no reason to complain of our slow pace here. The horses flew like lightning along the intervening path, and drew up at the door all panting, as if they had run a race. My wife stood waiting to receive me, with a pale face, and a candle in her hand, which made her look paler still as the wind blew the flame about. "He is sleeping," she said in a whisper, as if her voice might wake him. And I replied, when I could find my voice, also in a whisper, as though the jingling of the horses' furniture and the sound of their hoofs must not have been more dangerous. I stood on the steps with her a moment, almost afraid to go in, now that I was here; and it seemed to me that I saw without observing, if I may say so, that the horses were unwilling to turn round, though their stables lay that way, or that the men were unwilling. These things occurred to me afterwards, though at the moment I was not capable of anything but to ask questions and to hear of the condition of the boy.

I looked at him from the door of his room, for we were afraid to go near, lest we should disturb that blessed sleep. It looked like actual sleep, not the lethargy into which my wife told me he would sometimes fall. She told me everything in the next room, which communicated with his, rising now and then and going to the door of communication; and in this there was much that was very startling and confusing to the mind. It appeared that ever since the winter began—since it was early dark, and night had fallen before his return from school—he had been hearing voices among the ruins: at first only a groaning, he said, at which his pony was as much alarmed as he was, but by degrees a voice. The tears ran down my wife's cheeks as she described to me how he would start up in the night and cry out, "Oh, mother, let me in! oh, mother, let me in!" with a pathos which rent her heart. And she sitting there all the time, only longing to do everything his heart could desire! But though she would try to soothe him, crying, "You are at home, my darling. I am here. Don't you know me? Your mother is here!" he would only stare at her, and after a while spring up again with the same cry. At other times he would be quite reasonable, she said, asking eagerly when I was coming, but declaring that he must go with me as soon as I did so, "to let them in." "The doctor thinks his nervous system must have received a shock," my wife said. "Oh, Henry, can it be that we have pushed him on too much with his work—a delicate boy like Roland? And what is his work in comparison with his health? Even you would think little of honors or prizes if it hurt the boy's health." Even I!—as if I were an inhuman father sacrificing my child to my ambition. But I would not increase her trouble by taking any notice. After awhile they persuaded me to lie down, to rest, and to eat, none of which things had been possible since I received their letters. The mere fact of being on the spot, of course, in itself was a great thing; and when I knew that I could be called in a moment, as soon as he was awake and wanted me, I felt capable, even in the dark, chill morning twilight, to snatch an hour or two's sleep. As it happened, I was so worn out with the strain of anxiety, and he so quieted and consoled by knowing I had come, that I was not disturbed till the afternoon, when the twilight had again settled down. There was just daylight enough to see his face when I went to him; and what a change in a fortnight! He was paler and more worn, I thought, than even in those dreadful days in the plains before we left India. His hair seemed to me to have grown long and lank; his eyes were like blazing lights projecting out of his white face. He got hold of my hand in a cold and tremulous clutch, and waved to everybody to go away. "Go away—even mother," he said; "go away." This went to her heart; for she did not like that even I should have more of the boy's confidence than herself; but my wife has never been a woman to think of herself, and she left us alone. "Are they all gone?" he said eagerly. "They would not let me speak. The doctor treated me as if I were a fool. You know I am not a fool, papa."

"Yes, yes, my boy, I know. But you are ill, and quiet is so necessary. You are not only not a fool, Roland, but you are reasonable and understand. When you are ill you must deny yourself; you must not do everything that you might do being well."

He waved his thin hand with a sort of indignation. "Then, father, I am not ill," he cried. "Oh, I thought when you came you would not stop me,—you would see the sense of it! What do you think is the matter with me, all of you? Simson is well enough; but he is only a doctor. What do you think is the matter with me? I am no more ill than you are. A doctor, of course, he thinks you are ill the moment he looks at you—that's what he's there for—and claps you into bed."

"Which is the best place for you at present, my dear boy."

"I made up my mind," cried the little fellow, "that I would stand it till you came home. I said to myself, I won't frighten mother and the girls. But now, father," he cried, half jumping out of bed, "it's not illness: it's a secret."

His eyes shone so wildly, his face was so swept with strong feeling, that my heart sank within me. It could be nothing but fever that did it, and fever had been so fatal. I got him into my arms to put him back into bed. "Roland," I said, humoring the poor child, which I knew was the only way, "if you are going to tell me this secret to do any good, you know you must be quite quiet, and not excite yourself. If you excite yourself, I must not let you speak."

"Yes, father," said the boy. He was quiet directly, like a man, as if he quite understood. When I had laid him back on his pillow, he looked up at me with that grateful, sweet look with which children, when they are ill, break one's heart, the water coming into his eyes in his weakness. "I was sure as soon as you were here you would know what to do," he said.

"To be sure, my boy. Now keep quiet, and tell it all out like a man." To think I was telling lies to my own child! for I did it only to humor him, thinking, poor little fellow, his brain was wrong.

"Yes, father. Father, there is some one in the park—some one that has been badly used."

"Hush, my dear; you remember there is to be no excitement. Well, who is this somebody, and who has been ill-using him? We will soon put a stop to that."

"All," cried Roland, "but it is not so easy as you think. I don't know who it is. It is just a cry. Oh, if you could hear it! It gets into my head in my sleep. I heard it as clear—as clear; and they think that I am dreaming, or raving perhaps," the boy said, with a sort of disdainful smile.

This look of his perplexed me; it was less like fever than I thought. "Are you quite sure you have not dreamed it, Roland?" I said.

"Dreamed?—that!" He was springing up again when he suddenly bethought himself, and lay down flat, with the same sort of smile on his face. "The pony heard it, too," he said. "She jumped as if she had been shot. If I had not grasped at the reins—for I was frightened, father—"

"No shame to you, my boy," said I, though I scarcely knew why.

"If I hadn't held to her like a leech, she'd have pitched me over her head, and never drew breath till we were at the door. Did the pony dream it?" he said, with a soft disdain, yet indulgence for my foolishness. Then he added slowly, "It was only a cry the first time, and all the time before you went away. I wouldn't tell you, for it was so wretched to be frightened. I thought it might be a hare or a rabbit snared, and I went in the morning and looked; but there was nothing. It was after you went I heard it really first; and this is what he says." He raised himself on his elbow close to me, and looked me in the face: "'Oh, mother, let me in! oh, mother, let me in!'" As he said the words a mist came over his face, the mouth quivered, the soft features all melted and changed, and when he had ended these pitiful words, dissolved in a shower of heavy tears.

Was it a hallucination? Was it the fever of the brain? Was it the disordered fancy caused by great bodily weakness? How could I tell? I thought it wisest to accept it as if it were all true.

"This is very touching, Roland," I said.

"Oh, if you had just heard it, father! I said to myself, if father heard it he would do something; but mamma, you know, she's given over to Simson, and that fellow's a doctor, and never thinks of anything but clapping you into bed."

"We must not blame Simson for being a doctor, Roland."

"No, no," said my boy, with delightful toleration and indulgence; "oh, no; that's the good of him; that's what he's for; I know that. But you—you are different; you are just father; and you'll do something—directly, papa, directly; this very night."

"Surely," I said. "No doubt it is some little lost child."

He gave me a sudden, swift look, investigating my face as though to see whether, after all, this was everything my eminence as "father" came to,—no more than that. Then he got hold of my shoulder, clutching it with his thin hand. "Look here," he said, with a quiver in his voice; "suppose it wasn't—living at all!"

"My dear boy, how then could you have heard it?" I said.

He turned away from me with a pettish exclamation,—"As if you didn't know better than that!"

"Do you want to tell me it is a ghost?" I said.

Roland withdrew his hand; his countenance assumed an aspect of great dignity and gravity; a slight quiver remained about his lips. "Whatever it was—you always said we were not to call names. It was something—in trouble. Oh, father, in terrible trouble!"

"But, my boy," I said (I was at my wits' end), "if it was a child that was lost, or any poor human creature—but, Roland, what do you want me to do?"

"I should know if I was you," said the child eagerly. "That is what I always said to myself,—Father will know. Oh, papa, papa, to have to face it night after night, in such terrible, terrible trouble, and never to be able to do it any good! I don't want to cry; it's like a baby, I know; but what can I do else? Out there all by itself in the ruin, and nobody to help it! I can't bear it! I can't bear it!" cried my generous boy. And in his weakness he burst out, after many attempts to restrain it, into a great childish fit of sobbing and tears.

I do not know that I ever was in a greater perplexity, in my life; and afterwards, when I thought of it, there was something comic in it too. It is bad enough to find your child's mind possessed with the conviction that he has seen, or heard, a ghost; but that he should require you to go instantly and help that ghost was the most bewildering experience that had ever come my way. I am a sober man myself, and not superstitious—at least any more than everybody is superstitious. Of course I do not believe in ghosts; but I don't deny, any more than other people, that there are stories which I cannot pretend to understand. My blood got a sort of chill in my veins at the idea that Roland should be a ghost-seer; for that generally means a hysterical temperament and weak health, and all that men most hate and fear for their children. But that I should take up his ghost and right its wrongs, and save it from its trouble, was such a mission as was enough to confuse any man. I did my best to console my boy without giving any promise of this astonishing kind; but he was too sharp for me: he would have none of my caresses. With sobs breaking in at intervals upon his voice, and the rain-drops hanging on his eyelids, he yet returned to the charge.

"It will be there now!—it will be there all the night! Oh, think, papa,—think if it was me! I can't rest for thinking of it. Don't!" he cried, putting away my hand,—"don't! You go and help it, and mother can take care of me."

"But, Roland, what can I do?"

My boy opened his eyes, which were large with weakness and fever, and gave me a smile such, I think, as sick children only know the secret of. "I was sure you would know as soon as you came. I always said, Father will know. And mother," he cried, with a softening of repose upon his face, his limbs relaxing, his form sinking with a luxurious ease in his bed,—"mother can come and take care of me."

I called her, and saw him turn to her with the complete dependence of a child; and then I went away and left them, as perplexed a man as any in Scotland. I must say, however, I had this consolation, that my mind was greatly eased about Roland. He might be under a hallucination; but his head was clear enough, and I did not think him so ill as everybody else did. The girls were astonished even at the ease with which I took it. "How do you think he is?" they said in a breath, coming round me, laying hold of me. "Not half so ill as I expected," I said; "not very bad at all." "Oh, papa, you are a darling!" cried Agatha, kissing me, and crying upon my shoulder; while little Jeanie, who was as pale as Roland, clasped both her arms round mine, and could not speak at all. I knew nothing about it, not half so much as Simson; but they believed in me: they had a feeling that all would go right now. God is very good to you when your children look to you like that. It makes one humble, not proud. I was not worthy of it; and then I recollected that I had to act the part of a father to Roland's ghost,—which made me almost laugh, though I might just as well have cried. It was the strangest mission that ever was intrusted to mortal man.

It was then I remembered suddenly the looks of the men when they turned to take the brougham to the stables in the dark that morning. They had not liked it, and the horses had not liked it. I remembered that even in my anxiety about Roland I had heard them tearing along the avenue back to the stables, and had made a memorandum mentally that I must speak of it. It seemed to me that the best thing I could do was to go to the stables now and make a few inquiries. It is impossible to fathom the minds of rustics; there might be some devilry of practical joking, for anything I knew; or they might have some interest in getting up a bad reputation for the Brentwood avenue. It was getting dark by the time I went out, and nobody who knows the country will need to be told how black is the darkness of a November night under high laurel-bushes and yew-trees. I walked into the heart of the shrubberies two or three times, not seeing a step before me, till I came out upon the broader carriage-road, where the trees opened a little, and there was a faint gray glimmer of sky visible, under which the great limes and elms stood darkling like ghosts; but it grew black again as I approached the corner where the ruins lay. Both eyes and ears were on the alert, as may be supposed; but I could see nothing in the absolute gloom, and, so far as I can recollect, I heard nothing. Nevertheless there came a strong impression upon me that somebody was there. It is a sensation which most people have felt. I have seen when it has been strong enough to awake me out of sleep, the sense of some one looking at me. I suppose my imagination had been affected by Roland's story; and the mystery of the darkness is always full of suggestions. I stamped my feet violently on the gravel to rouse myself, and called out sharply, "Who's there?" Nobody answered, nor did I expect any one to answer, but the impression had been made. I was so foolish that I did not like to look back, but went sideways, keeping an eye on the gloom behind. It was with great relief that I spied the light in the stables, making a sort of oasis in the darkness. I walked very quickly into the midst of that lighted and cheerful place, and thought the clank of the groom's pail one of the pleasantest sounds I had ever heard. The coachman was the head of this little colony, and it was to his house I went to pursue my investigations. He was a native of the district, and had taken care of the place in the absence of the family for years; it was impossible but that he must know everything that was going on, and all the traditions of the place. The men, I could see, eyed me anxiously when I thus appeared at such an hour among them, and followed me with their eyes to Jarvis's house, where he lived alone with his old wife, their children being all married and out in the world. Mrs. Jarvis met me with anxious questions. How was the poor young gentleman? But the others knew, I could see by their faces, that not even this was the foremost thing in my mind.

"Noises?—ou ay, there'll be noises,—the wind in the trees, and the water soughing down the glen. As for tramps, Cornel, no, there's little o' that kind o' cattle about here; and Merran at the gate's a careful body." Jarvis moved about with some embarrassment from one leg to another as he spoke. He kept in the shade, and did not look at me more than he could help. Evidently his mind was perturbed, and he had reasons for keeping his own counsel. His wife sat by, giving him a quick look now and then, but saying nothing. The kitchen was very snug and warm and bright,—as different as could be from the chill and mystery of the night outside.

"I think you are trifling with me, Jarvis," I said.

"Triflin', Cornel? No me. What would I trifle for? If the deevil himsel was in the auld hoose, I have no interest in 't one way or another—"

"Sandy, hold your peace!" cried his wife imperatively.

"And what am I to hold my peace for, wi' the Cornel standing there asking a' thae questions? I'm saying, if the deevil himself-"

"And I'm telling ye hold your peace!" cried the woman, in great excitement. "Dark November weather and lang nichts, and us that ken a' we ken. How daur ye name—a name that shouldna be spoken?" She threw down her stocking and got up, also in great agitation. "I tellt ye you never could keep it. It's no a thing that will hide, and the haill toun kens as weel as you or me. Tell the Cornel straight out—or see, I'll do it. I dinna hold wi' your secrets, and a secret that the haill toun kens!" She snapped her fingers with an air of large disdain. As for Jarvis, ruddy and big as he was, he shrank to nothing before this decided woman. He repeated to her two or three times her own adjuration, "Hold your peace!" then, suddenly changing his tone, cried out, "Tell him then, confound ye! I'll wash my hands o't. If a' the ghosts in Scotland were in the auld hoose, is that ony concern o' mine?"

After this I elicited without much difficulty the whole story. In the opinion of the Jarvises, and of everybody about, the certainty that the place was haunted was beyond all doubt. As Sandy and his wife warmed to the tale, one tripping up another in their eagerness to tell everything, it gradually developed as distinct a superstition as I ever heard, and not without poetry and pathos. How long it was since the voice had been heard first, nobody could tell with certainty. Jarvis's opinion was that his father, who had been coachman at Brentwood before him, had never heard anything about it, and that the whole thing had arisen within the last ten years, since the complete dismantling of the old house; which was a wonderfully modern date for a tale so well authenticated. According to these witnesses, and to several whom I questioned afterwards, and who were all in perfect agreement, it was only in the months of November and

December that "the visitation" occurred. During these months, the darkest of the year, scarcely a night passed without the recurrence of these inexplicable cries. Nothing, it was said, had ever been seen,—at least, nothing that could be identified. Some people, bolder or more imaginative than the others, had seen the darkness moving, Mrs. Jarvis said, with unconscious poetry. It began when night fell, and continued, at intervals, till day broke. Very often it was only all inarticulate cry and moaning, but sometimes the words which had taken possession of my poor boy's fancy had been distinctly audible,—"Oh, mother, let me in!" The Jarvises were not aware that there had ever been any investigation into it. The estate of Brentwood had lapsed into the hands of a distant branch of the family, who had lived but little there; and of the many people who had taken it, as I had done, few had remained through two Decembers. And nobody had taken the trouble to make a very close examination into the facts. "No, no," Jarvis said, shaking his head, "No, no, Cornel. Wha wad set themsels up for a laughin'-stock to a' the country-side, making a wark about a ghost? Naebody believes in ghosts. It bid to be the wind in the trees, the last gentleman said, or some effec' o' the water wrastlin' among the rocks. He said it was a' quite easy explained; but he gave up the hoose. And when you cam, Cornel, we were awfu' anxious you should never hear. What for should I have spoiled the bargain and hairmed the property for no-thing?"

"Do you call my child's life nothing?" I said in the trouble of the moment, unable to restrain myself. "And instead of telling this all to me, you have told it to him,—to a delicate boy, a child unable to sift evidence or judge for himself, a tender-hearted young creature—"

I was walking about the room with an anger all the hotter that I felt it to be most likely quite unjust. My heart was full of bitterness against the stolid retainers of a family who were content to risk other people's children and comfort rather than let a house be empty. If I had been warned I might have taken precautions, or left the place, or sent Roland away, a hundred things which now I could not do; and here I was with my boy in a brain-fever, and his life, the most precious life on earth, hanging in the balance, dependent on whether or not I could get to the reason of a commonplace ghost-story! I paced about in high wrath, not seeing what I was to do; for to take Roland away, even if he were able to travel, would not settle his agitated mind; and I feared even that a scientific explanation of refracted sound or reverberation, or any other of the easy certainties with which we elder men are silenced, would have very little effect upon the boy.

"Cornel," said Jarvis solemnly, "and she'll bear me witness,—the young gentleman never heard a word from me—no, nor from either groom or gardener; I'll gie ye my word for that. In the first place, he's no a lad that invites ye to talk. There are some that are, and some that arena. Some will draw ye on, till ye've tellt them a' the clatter of the toun, and a' ye ken, and whiles mair. But Maister Roland, his mind's fu' of his books. He's aye civil and kind, and a fine lad; but no that sort. And ye see it's for a' our interest, Cornel, that you should stay at Brentwood. I took it upon me mysel to pass the word,—'No a syllable to Maister Roland, nor to the young leddies—no a syllable.' The women-servants, that have little reason to be out at night, ken little or nothing about it. And some think it grand to have a ghost so long as they're no in the way of coming across it. If you had been tellt the story to begin with, maybe ye would have thought so yourself."

This was true enough, though it did not throw any light upon my perplexity. If we had heard of it to start with, it is possible that all the family would have considered the possession of a ghost a distinct advantage. It is the fashion of the times. We never think what a risk it is to play with young imaginations, but cry out, in the fashionable jargon, "A ghost!—nothing else was wanted to make it perfect." I should not have been above this myself. I should have smiled, of course, at the idea of the ghost at all, but then to feel that it was mine would have pleased my vanity. Oh, yes, I claim no exemption. The girls would have been delighted. I could fancy their eagerness, their interest, and excitement. No; if we had been told, it would have done no good,—we should have made the bargain all the more eagerly, the fools that we are. "And there has been no attempt to investigate it," I said, "to see what it really is?"

"Eh, Cornel," said the coachman's wife, "wha would investigate, as ye call it, a thing that nobody believes in? Ye would be the laughin'-stock of a' the country-side, as my man says."

"But you believe in it," I said, turning upon her hastily. The woman was taken by surprise. She made a step backward out of my way.

"Lord, Cornel, how ye frichten a body! Me!—there's awfu' strange things in this world. An unlearned person doesna ken what to think. But the minister and the gentry they just laugh in your face. Inquire into the thing that is not! Na, na, we just let it be."

"Come with me, Jarvis," I said hastily, "and we'll make an attempt at least. Say nothing to the men or to anybody. I'll come back after dinner, and we'll make a serious attempt to see what it is, if it is anything. If I hear it,—which I doubt,—you may be sure I shall never rest till I make it out. Be ready for me about ten o'clock."

"Me, Cornel!" Jarvis said, in a faint voice. I had not been looking at him in my own preoccupation, but when I did so, I found that the greatest change had come over the fat and ruddy coachman. "Me, Cornel!" he repeated, wiping the perspiration from his brow. His ruddy face hung in flabby folds, his knees knocked together, his voice seemed half extinguished in his throat. Then he began to rub his hands and smile upon me in a deprecating, imbecile way. "There's nothing I wouldna do to pleasure ye, Cornel," taking a step further back. "I'm sure she kens I've aye said I never had to do with a mair fair, weel-spoken gentleman—" Here Jarvis came to a pause, again looking at me, rubbing his hands.

"Well?" I said.

"But eh, sir!" he went on, with the same imbecile yet insinuating smile, "if ye'll reflect that I am no used to my feet. With a horse atween my legs, or the reins in my hand, I'm maybe nae worse than other men; but on fit, Cornel—It's no the—bogles—but I've been cavalry, ye see," with a little hoarse laugh, "a' my life. To face a thing ye dinna understan'—on your feet, Cornel."

"Well, sir, if I do it," said I tartly, "why shouldn't you?"

"Eh, Cornel, there's an awfu' difference. In the first place, ye tramp about the haill countryside, and think naething of it; but a walk tires me mair than a hunard miles' drive; and then ye're a gentleman, and do your ain pleasure; and you're no so auld as me; and it's for your ain bairn, ye see, Cornel; and then—"

"He believes in it, Cornel, and you dinna believe in it," the woman said.

"Will you come with me?" I said, turning to her.

She jumped back, upsetting her chair in her bewilderment. "Me!" with a scream, and then fell into a sort of hysterical laugh. "I wouldna say but what I would go; but what would the folk say to hear of Cornel Mortimer with an auld silly woman at his heels?"

The suggestion made me laugh too, though I had little inclination for it. "I'm sorry you have so little spirit, Jarvis," I said. "I must find some one else, I suppose."

Jarvis, touched by this, began to remonstrate, but I cut him short. My butler was a soldier who had been with me in India, and was not supposed to fear anything,—man or devil,—certainly not the former; and I felt that I was losing time. The Jarvises were too thankful to get rid of me. They attended me to the door with the most anxious courtesies. Outside, the two grooms stood close by, a little confused by my sudden exit. I don't know if perhaps they had been listening,—at least standing as near as possible, to catch any scrap of the conversation. I waved my hand to them as

I went past, in answer to their salutations, and it was very apparent to me that they also were glad to see me go.

And it will be thought very strange, but it would be weak not to add, that I myself, though bent on the investigation I have spoken of, pledged to Roland to carry it out, and feeling that my boy's health, perhaps his life, depended on the result of my inquiry,—I felt the most unaccountable reluctance to pass these ruins on my way home. My curiosity was intense; and yet it was all my mind could do to pull my body along. I daresay the scientific people would describe it the other way, and attribute my cowardice to the state of my stomach. I went on; but if I had followed my impulse, I should have turned and bolted. Everything in me seemed to cry out against it: my heart thumped, my pulses all began, like sledge-hammers, beating against my ears and every sensitive part. It was very dark, as I have said; the old house, with its shapeless tower, loomed a heavy mass through the darkness, which was only not entirely so solid as itself. On the other hand, the great dark cedars of which we were so proud seemed to fill up the night. My foot strayed out of the path in my confusion and the gloom together, and I brought myself up with a cry as I felt myself knock against something solid. What was it? The contact with hard stone and lime and prickly bramble-bushes restored me a little to myself. "Oh, it's only the old gable," I said aloud, with a little laugh to reassure myself. The rough feeling of the stones reconciled me. As I groped about thus, I shook off my visionary folly. What so easily explained as that I should have strayed from the path in the darkness? This brought me back to common existence, as if I had been shaken by a wise hand out of all the silliness of superstition. How silly it was, after all! What did it matter which path I took? I laughed again, this time with better heart, when suddenly, in a moment, the blood was chilled in my veins, a shiver stole along my spine, my faculties seemed to forsake me. Close by me, at my side, at my feet, there was a sigh. No, not a groan, not a moaning, not anything so tangible,—a perfectly soft, faint, inarticulate sigh. I sprang back, and my heart stopped beating. Mistaken! no, mistake was impossible. I heard it as clearly as I hear myself speak; a long, soft, weary sigh, as if drawn to the utmost, and emptying out a load of sadness that filled the breast. To hear this in the solitude, in the dark, in the night (though it was still early), had an effect which I cannot describe. I feel it now,—something cold creeping over me, up into my hair, and down to my feet, which refused to move. I cried out, with a trembling voice, "Who is there?" as I had done before; but there was no reply.

I got home I don't quite know how; but in my mind there was no longer any indifference as to the thing, whatever it was, that haunted these ruins. My scepticism disappeared like a mist. I was as firmly determined that there was something as Roland was. I did not for a moment pretend to myself that it was possible I could be deceived; there were movements and noises which I understood all about,—cracklings of small branches in the frost, and little rolls of gravel on the path, such as have a very eerie sound sometimes, and perplex you with wonder as to who has done it, when there is no real mystery; but I assure you all these little movements of nature don't affect you one bit when there is something. I understood them. I did not understand the sigh. That was not simple nature; there was meaning in it, feeling, the soul of a creature invisible. This is the thing that human nature trembles at,—a creature invisible, yet with sensations, feelings, a power somehow of expressing itself. I had not the same sense of unwillingness to turn my back upon the scene of the mystery which I had experienced in going to the stables; but I almost ran home, impelled by eagerness to get everything done that had to be done, in order to apply myself to finding it out. Bagley was in the hall as usual when I went in. He was always there in the afternoon, always with the appearance of perfect occupation, yet, so far as I know, never doing anything. The door was open, so that I hurried in without any pause, breathless; but the sight of his calm regard, as he came to help me off with my overcoat, subdued me in a moment. Anything out of the way, anything incomprehensible, faded to nothing in the presence of Bagley. You saw and wondered how he was made: the parting of his hair, the tie of his white neckcloth, the fit of his trousers, all perfect as works of art; but you could see how they were done, which makes all the difference. I flung myself upon him, so to speak, without waiting to note the extreme unlikeness of the man to anything of the kind I meant. "Bagley," I said, "I want you to come out with me to-night to watch for—"

"Poachers, Colonel?" he said, a gleam of pleasure running all over him.

"No, Bagley; a great deal worse," I cried.

"Yes, Colonel; at what hour, sir?" the man said; but then I had not told him what it was.

It was ten o'clock when we set out. All was perfectly quiet indoors. My wife was with Roland, who had been quite calm, she said, and who (though, no doubt, the fever must run its course) had been better ever since I came. I told Bagley to put on a thick greatcoat over his evening coat, and did the same myself, with strong boots; for the soil was like a sponge, or worse. Talking to him, I almost forgot what we were going to do. It was darker even than it had been before, and Bagley kept very close to me as we went along. I had a small lantern in my hand, which gave us a partial guidance. We had come to the corner where the path turns. On one side was the bowling-green, which the girls had taken possession of for their croquet-ground,—a wonderful enclosure surrounded by high hedges of holly, three hundred years old and more; on the other, the ruins. Both were black as night; but before we got so far, there was a little opening in which we could just discern the trees and the lighter line of the road. I thought it best to pause there and take breath. "Bagley," I said, "there is something about these ruins I don't understand. It is there I am going. Keep your eyes open and your wits about you. Be ready to pounce upon any stranger you see,—anything, man or woman. Don't hurt, but seize anything you see." "Colonel," said Bagley, with a little tremor in his breath, "they do say there's things there—as is neither man nor woman." There was no time for words. "Are you game to follow me, my man? that's the question," I said. Bagley fell in without a word, and saluted. I knew then I had nothing to fear.

We went, so far as I could guess, exactly as I had come; when I heard that sigh. The darkness, however, was so complete that all marks, as of trees or paths, disappeared. One moment we felt our feet on the gravel, another sinking noiselessly into the slippery grass, that was all. I had shut up my lantern, not wishing to scare any one, whoever it might be. Bagley followed, it seemed to me, exactly in my footsteps as I made my way, as I supposed, towards the mass of the ruined house. We seemed to take a long time groping along seeking this; the squash of the wet soil under our feet was the only thing that marked our progress. After a while I stood still to see, or rather feel, where we were. The darkness was very still, but no stiller than is usual in a winter's night. The sounds I have mentioned—the crackling of twigs, the roll of a pebble, the sound of some rustle in the dead leaves, or creeping creature on the grass—were audible when you listened, all mysterious enough when your mind is disengaged, but to me cheering now as signs of the livingness of nature, even in the death of the frost. As we stood still there came up from the trees in the glen the prolonged hoot of an owl. Bagley started with alarm, being in a state of general nervousness, and not knowing what he was afraid of. But to me the sound was encouraging and pleasant, being so comprehensible.

"An owl," I said, under my breath. "Y—es, Colonel," said Bagley, his teeth chattering. We stood still about five minutes, while it broke into the still brooding of the air, the sound widening out in circles, dying upon the darkness. This sound, which is not a cheerful one, made me almost gay. It was natural, and relieved the tension of the mind. I moved on with new courage, my nervous excitement calming down.

When all at once, quite suddenly, close to us, at our feet, there broke out a cry. I made a spring backwards in the first moment of surprise and horror, and in doing so came sharply against the same rough masonry and brambles that had struck me before. This new sound came upwards from the ground,—a low, moaning, wailing voice, full of suffering and pain. The contrast between it and the hoot of the owl was indescribable,—the one with a wholesome wildness and naturalness that hurt nobody; the other, a sound that made one's blood curdle, full of human misery. With a great deal of fumbling,—for in spite of everything I could do to keep up my courage my hands shook,—I managed to remove the slide of my lantern. The light leaped out like something living, and made the place visible in a moment. We were what would have been inside the ruined building had anything remained but the gable-wall which I have described. It was close to us, the vacant door-way in it going out straight into the blackness outside. The light showed the bit of wall, the ivy glistening upon it in clouds of dark green, the bramble-branches waving, and below, the open door,—a door that led to nothing. It was from this the voice came which died out just as the light flashed upon this strange scene. There was a moment's silence, and then it broke forth again. The sound was so near, so penetrating, so pitiful, that, in the nervous start I gave, the light fell out of my hand. As I groped for it in the dark my hand was clutched by Bagley, who, I think, must have dropped upon his knees; but I was too much perturbed myself to think much of this. He clutched at me in the confusion of his terror, forgetting all his usual decorum. "For God's sake, what is it, sir?" he gasped. If I yielded, there was evidently an end of both of us. "I can't tell," I said, "any more than you; that's what we've got to find out. Up, man, up!" I pulled him to his feet. "Will you go round and examine the other side, or will you stay here with the lantern?" Bagley gasped at me with a face of horror. "Can't we stay together, Colonel?" he said; his knees were trembling under him. I pushed him against the corner of the wall, and put the light into his hands. "Stand fast till I come back; shake yourself together, man; let nothing pass you," I said. The voice was within two or three feet of us; of that there could be no doubt.

I went myself to the other side of the wall, keeping close to it. The light shook in Bagley's hand, but, tremulous though it was, shone out through the vacant door, one oblong block of light marking all the crumbling corners and hanging masses of foliage. Was that something dark huddled in a heap by the side of it? I pushed forward across the light in the door-way, and fell upon it with my hands; but it was only a juniper-bush growing close against the wall. Meanwhile, the sight of my figure crossing the door-way had brought Bagley's nervous excitement to a height: he flew at me, gripping my shoulder. "I've got him, Colonel! I've got him!" he cried, with a voice of sudden exultation. He thought it was a man, and was at once relieved. But at that moment the voice burst forth again between us, at our feet,—more close to us than any separate being could be. He dropped off from me, and fell against the wall, his jaw dropping as if he were dying. I suppose, at the same moment, he saw that it was me whom he had clutched. I, for my part, had scarcely more command of myself. I snatched the light out of his hand, and flashed it all about me wildly. Nothing,—the juniper-bush which I thought I had never seen before, the heavy growth of the glistening ivy, the brambles waving. It was close to my ears now, crying, crying, pleading as if for life. Either I heard the same words Roland had heard, or else, in my excitement, his imagination got possession of mine. The voice went on, growing into distinct articulation, but wavering about, now from one point, now from another, as if the owner of it were moving slowly back and forward. "Mother! mother!" and then an outburst of wailing. As my mind steadied, getting accustomed (as one's mind gets accustomed to anything), it seemed to me as if some uneasy, miserable creature was pacing up and down before a closed door. Sometimes—but that must have been excitement—I thought I heard a sound like knocking, and then another burst, "Oh, mother! mother!" All this close, close to the space where I was standing with my lantern, now before me, now behind me: a creature restless, unhappy, moaning, crying, before the vacant door-way, which no one could either shut or open more.

"Do you hear it, Bagley? do you hear what it is saying?" I cried, stepping in through the door-way. He was lying against the wall, his eyes glazed, half dead with terror. He made a motion of his lips as if to answer me, but no sounds came; then lifted his hand with a curious imperative movement as if ordering me to be silent and listen. And how long I did so I cannot tell. It began to have an interest, an exciting hold upon me, which I could not describe. It seemed to call up visibly a scene any one could understand,—a something shut out, restlessly wandering to and fro; sometimes the voice dropped, as if throwing itself down, sometimes wandered off a few paces, growing sharp and clear. "Oh, mother, let me in! oh, mother, mother, let me in! oh, let me in!" Every word was clear to me. No wonder the boy had gone wild with pity. I tried to steady my mind upon Roland, upon his conviction that I could do something, but my head swam with the excitement, even when I partially overcame the terror. At last the words died away, and there was a sound of sobs and moaning. I cried out, "In the name of God, who are you?" with a kind of feeling in my mind that to use the name of God was profane, seeing that I did not believe in ghosts or anything supernatural; but I did it all the same, and waited, my heart giving a leap of terror lest there should be a reply. Why this should have been I cannot tell, but I had a feeling that if there was an answer it would be more than I could bear. But there was no answer; the moaning went on, and then, as if it had been real, the voice rose a little higher again, the words recommenced, "Oh, mother, let me in! oh, mother, let me in!" with an expression that was heart-breaking to hear.

As if it had been real! What do I mean by that? I suppose I got less alarmed as the thing went on. I began to recover the use of my senses,—I seemed to explain it all to myself by saying that this had once happened, that it was a recollection of a real scene. Why there should have seemed something quite satisfactory and composing in this explanation I cannot tell, but so it was. I began to listen almost as if it had been a play, forgetting Bagley, who, I almost think, had fainted, leaning against the wall. I was startled out of this strange spectatorship that had fallen upon me by the sudden rush of something which made my heart jump once more, a large black figure in the door-way waving its arms. "Come in! come in! come in!" it shouted out hoarsely at the top of a deep bass voice, and then poor Bagley fell down senseless across the threshold. He was less sophisticated than I,—he had not been able to bear it any longer. I took him for something supernatural, as he took me, and it was some time before I awoke to the necessities of the moment. I remembered only after, that from the time I began to give my attention to the man, I heard the other voice no more. It was some time before I brought him to. It must have been a strange scene: the lantern making a luminous spot in the darkness, the man's white face lying on the black earth, I over him, doing what I could for him, probably I should have been thought to be murdering him had any one seen us. When at last I succeeded in pouring a little brandy down his throat, he sat up and looked about him wildly. "What's up?" he said; then recognizing me, tried to struggle to his feet with a faint "Beg your pardon, Colonel." I got him home as best I could, making him lean upon my arm. The great fellow was as weak as a child. Fortunately he did not for some time remember what had happened. From the time Bagley fell the voice had stopped, and all was still.

"You've got an epidemic in your house, Colonel," Simson said to me next morning. "What's the meaning of it all? Here's your butler raving about a voice. This will never do, you know; and so far as I can make out, you are in it too."

"Yes, I am in it, Doctor. I thought I had better speak to you. Of course you are treating Roland all right, but the boy is not raving, he is as sane as you or me. It's all true."

"As sane as—I—or you. I never thought the boy insane. He's got cerebral excitement, fever. I don't know what you've got. There's something very queer about the look of your eyes."

"Come," said I, "you can't put us all to bed, you know. You had better listen and hear the symptoms in full."

The Doctor shrugged his shoulders, but he listened to me patiently. He did not believe a word of the story, that was clear; but he heard it all from beginning to end. "My dear fellow," he said, "the boy told me just the same. It's an epidemic. When one person falls a victim to this sort of thing, it's as safe as can be,—there's always two or three."

"Then how do you account for it?" I said.

"Oh, account for it!—that's a different matter; there's no accounting for the freaks our brains are subject to. If it's delusion, if it's some trick of the echoes or the winds,—some phonetic disturbance or other—"

"Come with me to-night, and judge for yourself," I said.

Upon this he laughed aloud, then said, "That's not such a bad idea; but it would ruin me forever if it were known that John Simson was ghost-hunting."

"There it is," said I; "you dart down on us who are unlearned with your phonetic disturbances, but you daren't examine what the thing really is for fear of being laughed at. That's science!"

"It's not science,—it's common-sense," said the Doctor. "The thing has delusion on the front of it. It is encouraging an unwholesome tendency even to examine. What good could come of it? Even if I am convinced, I shouldn't believe."

"I should have said so yesterday; and I don't want you to be convinced or to believe," said I. "If you prove it to be a delusion, I shall be very much obliged to you for one. Come; somebody must go with me."

"You are cool," said the Doctor. "You've disabled this poor fellow of yours, and made him—on that point—a lunatic for life; and now you want to disable me. But, for once, I'll do it. To save appearance, if you'll give me a bed, I'll come over after my last rounds."

It was agreed that I should meet him at the gate, and that we should visit the scene of last night's occurrences before we came to the house, so that nobody might be the wiser. It was scarcely possible to hope that the cause of Bagley's sudden illness should not somehow steal into the knowledge of the servants at least, and it was better that all should be done as quietly as possible. The day seemed to me a very long one. I had to spend a certain part of it with Roland, which was a terrible ordeal for me, for what could I say to the boy? The improvement continued, but he was still in a very precarious state, and the trembling vehemence with which he turned to me when his mother left the room filled me with alarm. "Father?" he said quietly. "Yes, my boy, I am giving my best attention to it; all is being done that I can do. I have not come to any conclusion—yet. I am neglecting nothing you said," I cried. What I could not do was to give his active mind any encouragement to dwell upon the mystery. It was a hard predicament, for some satisfaction had to be given him. He looked at me very wistfully, with the great blue eyes which shone so large and brilliant out of his white and worn face. "You must trust me," I said. "Yes, father. Father understands," he said to himself, as if to soothe some inward doubt. I left him as soon as I could. He was about the most precious thing I had on earth, and his health my first thought; but yet somehow, in the excitement of this other subject, I put that aside, and preferred not to dwell upon Roland, which was the most curious part of it all.

That night at eleven I met Simson at the gate. He had come by train, and I let him in gently myself. I had been so much absorbed in the coming experiment that I passed the ruins in going to meet him, almost without thought, if you can understand that. I had my lantern; and he showed me a coil of taper which he had ready for use. "There is nothing like light," he said, in his scoffing tone. It was a very still night, scarcely a sound, but not so dark. We could keep the path without difficulty as we went along. As we approached the spot we could hear a low moaning, broken occasionally by a bitter cry. "Perhaps that is your voice," said the Doctor; "I thought it must be something of the kind. That's a poor brute caught in some of these infernal traps of yours; you'll find it among the bushes somewhere." I said nothing. I felt no particular fear, but a triumphant satisfaction in what was to follow. I led him to the spot where Bagley and I had stood on the previous night. All was silent as a winter night could be,—so silent that we heard far off the sound of the horses in the stables, the shutting of a window at the house. Simson lighted his taper and went peering about, poking into all the corners. We looked like two conspirators lying in wait for some unfortunate traveller; but not a sound broke the quiet. The moaning had stopped before we came up; a star or two shone over us in the sky, looking down as if surprised at our strange proceedings. Dr. Simson did nothing but utter subdued laughs under his breath. "I thought as much," he said. "It is just the same with tables and all other kinds of ghostly apparatus; a sceptic's presence stops everything. When I am present nothing ever comes off. How long do you think it will be necessary to stay here? Oh, I don't complain; only when you are satisfied, I am—quite."

I will not deny that I was disappointed beyond measure by this result. It made me look like a credulous fool. It gave the Doctor such a pull over me as nothing else could. I should point all his morals for years to come; and his materialism, his scepticism, would be increased beyond endurance. "It seems, indeed," I said, "that there is to be no—" "Manifestation," he said, laughing; "that is what all the mediums say. No manifestations, in consequence of the presence of an unbeliever." His laugh sounded very uncomfortable to me in the silence; and it was now near midnight. But that laugh seemed the signal; before it died away the moaning we had heard before was resumed. It started from some distance off, and came towards us, nearer and nearer, like some one walking along and moaning to himself. There could be no idea now that it was a hare caught in a trap. The approach was slow, like that of a weak person, with little halts and pauses. We heard it coming along the grass straight towards the vacant door-way. Simson had been a little startled by the first sound. He said hastily, "That child has no business to be out so late." But he felt, as well as I, that this was no child's voice. As it came nearer, he grew silent, and, going to the door-way with his taper, stood looking out towards the sound. The taper being unprotected blew about in the night air, though there was scarcely any wind. I threw the light of my lantern steady and white across the same space. It was in a blaze of light in the midst of the blackness. A little icy thrill had gone over me at the first sound, but as it came close, I confess that my only feeling was satisfaction. The scoffer could scoff no more. The light touched his own face, and showed a very perplexed countenance. If he was afraid, he concealed it with great success, but he was perplexed. And then all that had happened on the previous night was enacted once more. It fell strangely upon me with a sense of repetition. Every cry, every sob seemed the same as before. I listened almost without any emotion at all in my own person, thinking of its effect upon Simson. He maintained a very bold front, on the whole. All that coming and going of the voice was, if our ears could be trusted, exactly in front of the vacant, blank door-way, blazing full of light, which caught and shone in the glistening leaves of the great hollies at a little distance. Not a rabbit could have crossed the turf without being seen; but there was nothing. After a time, Simson, with a certain caution and bodily reluctance, as it seemed to me, went out with his roll of taper into this space. His figure showed against the holly in full outline. Just at this moment the voice sank, as was its custom, and seemed to fling itself down at the door. Simson recoiled violently, as if some one had come up against him, then turned, and held his taper low, as if examining something. "Do you see anybody?" I cried in a whisper, feeling the chill of nervous panic steal over me at this action. "It's nothing but a—confounded juniper-bush," he said. This I knew very well to be nonsense, for the juniper-bush was on the other side. He went about after this round and round, poking his taper everywhere, then returned to me on the inner side of the wall. He scoffed no longer; his face was contracted and pale. "How long does this go on?" he whispered to me, like a man who does not wish to interrupt some one who is speaking. I had become too much perturbed myself to remark whether the successions and changes of the voice were the same as last night. It suddenly went out in the air almost as he was speaking, with a soft reiterated sob dying away. If there had been anything to be seen, I should have said that the person was at that moment crouching on the ground close to the door.

We walked home very silent afterwards. It was only when we were in sight of the house that I said, "What do you think of it?" "I can't tell what to think of it," he said quickly. He took—though he was a very temperate man—not the claret I was going to offer him, but some brandy from the tray, and swallowed it almost undiluted. "Mind you, I don't believe a word of it," he said, when he had lighted his candle; "but I can't tell what to think," he turned round to add, when he was half-way upstairs.

All of this, however, did me no good with the solution of my problem. I was to help this weeping, sobbing thing, which was already to me as distinct a personality as anything I knew; or what should I say to Roland? It was on my heart that my boy would die if I could not find some way of helping this creature. You may be surprised that I should speak of it in this way. I did not know if it was man or woman; but I no more doubted that it was a soul in pain than I doubted my own being; and it was my business to soothe this pain,—to deliver it, if that was possible. Was ever such a task given to an anxious father trembling for his only boy? I felt in my heart, fantastic as it may appear, that I must fulfill this somehow, or part with my child; and you may conceive that rather than do that I was ready to die. But even my dying would not have advanced me, unless by bringing me into the same world with that seeker at the door.

Next morning Simson was out before breakfast, and came in with evident signs of the damp grass on his boots, and a look of worry and weariness, which did not say much for the night he had passed. He improved a little after breakfast, and visited his two patients,—for Bagley was still an invalid. I went out with him on his way to the train, to hear what he had to say about the boy. "He is going on very well," he said; "there are no complications as yet. But mind you, that's not a boy to be trifled with, Mortimer. Not a word to him about last night." I had to tell him then of my last interview with Roland, and of the impossible demand he had made upon me, by which, though he tried to laugh, he was much discomposed, as I could see. "We must just perjure ourselves all round," he said, "and swear you exorcised it;" but the man was too kind-hearted to be satisfied with that. "It's frightfully serious for you, Mortimer. I can't laugh as I should like to. I wish I saw a way out of it, for your sake. By the way," he added shortly, "didn't you notice that juniper-bush on the left-hand side?" "There was one on the right hand of the door. I noticed you made that mistake last night." "Mistake!" he cried, with a curious low laugh, pulling up the collar of his coat as though he felt the cold,—"there's no juniper there this morning, left or right. Just go and see." As he stepped into the train a few minutes after, he looked back upon me and beckoned me for a parting word. "I'm coming back to-night," he said.

I don't think I had any feeling about this as I turned away from that common bustle of the railway which made my private preoccupations feel so strangely out of date. There had been a distinct satisfaction in my mind before, that his scepticism had been so entirely defeated. But the more serious part of the matter pressed upon me now. I went straight from the railway to the manse, which stood on a little plateau on the side of the river opposite to the woods of Brentwood. The minister was one of a class which is not so common in Scotland as it used to be. He was a man of good family, well educated in the Scotch way, strong in philosophy, not so strong in Greek, strongest of all in experience,—a man who had "come across," in the course of his life, most people of note that had ever been in Scotland, and who was said to be very sound in doctrine, without infringing the toleration with which old men, who are good men, are generally endowed. He was old-fashioned; perhaps he did not think so much about the troublous problems of theology as many of the young men, nor ask himself any hard questions about the Confession of Faith; but he understood human nature, which is perhaps better. He received me with a cordial welcome.

"Come away, Colonel Mortimer," he said; "I'm all the more glad to see you, that I feel it's a good sign for the boy. He's doing well?—God be praised,—and the Lord bless him and keep him. He has many a poor body's prayers, and that can do nobody harm."

"He will need them all, Dr. Moncrieff," I said, "and your counsel too." And I told him the story,—more than I had told Simson. The old clergyman listened to me with many suppressed exclamations, and at the end the water stood in his eyes.

"That's just beautiful," he said. "I do not mind to have heard anything like it; it's as fine as Burns when he wished deliverance to one—that is prayed for in no kirk. Ay, ay! so he would have you console the poor lost spirit? God bless the boy! There's something more than common in that, Colonel Mortimer. And also the faith of him in his father!—I would like to put that into a sermon." Then the old gentleman gave me an alarmed look, and said, "No, no; I was not meaning a sermon; but I must write it down for the 'Children's Record.'" I saw the thought that passed through his mind. Either he thought, or he feared I would think, of a funeral sermon. You may believe this did not make me more cheerful.

I can scarcely say that Dr. Moncrieff gave me any advice. How could any one advise on such a subject? But he said, "I think I'll come too. I'm an old man; I'm less liable to be frightened than those that are further off the world unseen. It behooves me to think of my own journey there. I've no cut-and-dry beliefs on the subject. I'll come too; and maybe at the moment the Lord will put into our heads what to do."

This gave me a little comfort,—more than Simson had given me. To be clear about the cause of it was not my grand desire. It was another thing that was in my mind,—my boy. As for the poor soul at the open door, I had no more doubt, as I have said, of its existence than I had of my own. It was no ghost to me. I knew the creature, and it was in trouble. That was my feeling about it, as it was Roland's. To hear it first was a great shock to my nerves, but not now; a man will get accustomed to anything. But to do something for it was the great problem; how was I to be serviceable to a being that was invisible, that was mortal no longer? "Maybe at the moment the Lord will put it into our heads." This is very old-fashioned phraseology, and a week before, most likely, I should have smiled (though always with kindness) at Dr. Moncrieff's credulity; but there was a great comfort, whether rational or otherwise I cannot say, in the mere sound of the words.

The road to the station and the village lay through the glen, not by the ruins; but though the sunshine and the fresh air, and the beauty of the trees, and the sound of the water were all very soothing to the spirits, my mind was so full of my own subject that I could not refrain from turning to the right hand as I got to the top of the glen, and going straight to the place which I may call the scene of all my thoughts. It was lying full in the sunshine, like all the rest of the world. The ruined gable looked due east, and in the present aspect of the sun the light streamed down through the door-way as our lantern had done, throwing a flood of light upon the damp grass beyond. There was a strange suggestion in the open door,—so futile, a kind of emblem of vanity: all free around, so that you could go where you pleased, and yet that semblance of an enclosure,—that way of entrance, unnecessary, leading to nothing. And why any creature should pray and weep to get in—to nothing, or be kept out—by nothing, you could not dwell upon it, or it made your brain go round. I remembered, however, what Simson said about the juniper, with a little smile on my own mind as to the inaccuracy of recollection which even a scientific man will be guilty of. I could see now the light of my lantern gleaming upon the wet glistening surface of the spiky leaves at the right hand,—and he ready to go to the stake for it that it was the left! I went round to make sure. And then I saw what he had said. Right or left there was no juniper at all! I was confounded by this, though it was entirely a matter of detail nothing at all,—a bush of brambles waving, the grass growing up to the very walls. But after all, though it gave me a shock for a moment, what did that matter? There were marks as if a number of footsteps had been up and down in front of the door, but these might have been our steps; and all was bright and peaceful and still. I poked about the other ruin—the larger ruins of the old house—for some time, as I had done before. There were marks upon the grass here and there—I could not call them footsteps—all about; but that told for nothing one way or another. I had examined the ruined rooms closely the first day. They were half filled up with soil and debris, withered brackens and bramble,—no refuge for any one there. It vexed me that Jarvis should see me coming from that spot when he came up to me for his orders. I don't know whether my nocturnal expeditions had got wind among the servants, but there was a significant look in his face. Something in it I felt was like my own sensation when Simson in the midst of his scepticism was struck dumb. Jarvis felt satisfied that his veracity had been put beyond question. I never spoke to a servant of mine in such a peremptory tone before. I sent him away "with a flea in his lug," as the man described it afterwards. Interference of any kind was intolerable to me at such a moment.

But what was strangest of all was, that I could not face Roland. I did not go up to his room, as I would have naturally done, at once. This the girls could not understand. They saw there was some mystery in it. "Mother has gone to lie down," Agatha said; "he has had such a good night." "But he wants you so, papa!" cried little Jeanie, always with her two arms embracing mine in a pretty way she had. I was obliged to go at last, but what could I say? I could only kiss him, and tell him to keep still,—that I was doing all I could. There is something mystical about the patience of a child. "It will come all right, won't it, father?" he said. "God grant it may! I hope so, Roland." "Oh, yes, it will come all right." Perhaps he understood that in the midst of my anxiety I could not stay with him as I should have done otherwise. But the girls were more surprised than it is possible to describe. They looked at me with wondering eyes. "If I were ill, papa, and you only stayed with me a moment, I should break my heart," said Agatha. But the boy had a sympathetic feeling. He knew that of my own will I would not have done it. I shut myself up in the library, where I could not rest, but kept pacing up and down like a caged beast. What could I do? and if I could do nothing, what would become of my boy? These were the questions that, without ceasing, pursued each other through my mind.

Simson came out to dinner, and when the house was all still, and most of the servants in bed, we went out and met Dr. Moncrieff, as we had appointed, at the head of the glen. Simson, for his part, was disposed to scoff at the Doctor. "If there are to be any spells, you know, I'll cut the whole concern," he said. I did not make him any reply. I had not invited him; he could go or come as he pleased. He was very talkative, far more so than suited my humor, as we went on. "One thing is certain, you know; there must be some human agency," he said. "It is all bosh about apparitions. I never have investigated the laws of sound to any great extent, and there's a great deal in ventriloquism that we don't know much about." "If it's the same to you," I said, "I wish you'd keep all that to yourself, Simson. It doesn't suit my state of mind." "Oh, I hope I know how to respect idiosyncrasy," he said. The very tone of his voice irritated me beyond measure. These scientific fellows, I wonder people put up with them as they do, when you have no mind for their cold-blooded confidence. Dr. Moncrieff met us about eleven o'clock, the same time as on the previous night. He was a large man, with a venerable countenance and white hair,—old, but in full vigor, and thinking less of a cold night walk than many a younger man. He had his lantern, as I had. We were fully provided with means of lighting the place, and we were all of us resolute men. We had a rapid consultation as we went up, and the result was that we divided to different posts. Dr. Moncrieff remained inside the wall—if you can call that inside where there was no wall but one. Simson placed himself on the side next the ruins, so as to intercept any communication with the old house, which was what his mind was fixed upon. I was posted on the other side. To say that nothing could come near without being seen was self-evident. It had been so also on the previous night. Now, with our three lights in the midst of the darkness, the whole place seemed illuminated. Dr. Moncrieff's lantern, which was a large one, without any means of shutting up,—an old-fashioned lantern with a pierced and ornamental top,—shone steadily, the rays shooting out of it upward into the gloom. He placed it on the grass, where the middle of the room, if this had been a room, would have been. The usual effect of the light streaming out of the door-way was prevented by the illumination which Simson and I on either side supplied. With these differences, everything seemed as on the previous night.

And what occurred was exactly the same, with the same air of repetition, point for point, as I had formerly remarked. I declare that it seemed to me as if I were pushed against, put aside, by the owner of the voice as he paced up and down in his trouble,—though these are perfectly futile words, seeing that the stream of light from my lantern, and that from Simson's taper, lay broad and clear, without a shadow, without the smallest break, across the entire breadth of the grass. I had ceased even to be alarmed, for my part. My heart was rent with pity and trouble,—pity for the poor suffering human creature that moaned and pleaded so, and trouble for myself and my boy. God! if I could not find any help,—and what help could I find?—Roland would die.

We were all perfectly still till the first outburst was exhausted, as I knew, by experience, it would be. Dr. Moncrieff, to whom it was new, was quite motionless on the other side of the wall, as we were in our places. My heart had remained almost at its usual beating during the voice. I was used to it; it did not rouse all my pulses as it did at first. But just as it threw itself sobbing at the door (I cannot use other words), there suddenly came something which sent the blood coursing through my veins, and my heart into my mouth. It was a voice inside the wall,—the minister's well-known voice. I would have been prepared for it in any kind of adjuration, but I was not prepared for what I heard. It came out with a sort of stammering, as if too much moved for utterance. "Willie, Willie! Oh, God preserve us! is it you?"

These simple words had an effect upon me that the voice of the invisible creature had ceased to have. I thought the old man, whom I had brought into this danger, had gone mad with terror. I made a dash round to the other side of the wall, half crazed myself with the thought. He was standing where I had left him, his shadow thrown vague and large upon the grass by the lantern which stood at his feet. I lifted my own light to see his face as I rushed forward. He was very pale, his eyes wet and glistening, his mouth quivering with parted lips. He neither saw nor heard me. We that had gone through this experience before, had crouched towards each other to get a little strength to bear it. But he was not even aware that I was there. His whole being seemed absorbed in anxiety and tenderness. He held out his hands, which trembled, but it seemed to me with eagerness, not fear. He went on speaking all the time. "Willie, if it is you,—and it's you, if it is not a delusion of Satan,—Willie, lad! why come ye here frighting them that know you not? Why came ye not to me?"

He seemed to wait for an answer. When his voice ceased, his countenance, every line moving, continued to speak. Simson gave me another terrible shock, stealing into the open door-way with his light, as much awe-stricken, as wildly curious, as I. But the minister resumed, without seeing Simson, speaking to some one else. His voice took a tone of expostulation:—

"Is this right to come here? Your mother's gone with your name on her lips. Do you think she would ever close her door on her own lad? Do ye think the Lord will close the door, ye faint-hearted creature? No!—I forbid ye! I forbid ye!" cried the old man. The sobbing voice had begun to resume its cries. He made a step forward, calling out the last words in a voice of command. "I forbid ye! Cry out no more to man. Go home, ye wandering spirit! go home! Do you hear me?—me that christened ye, that have struggled with ye, that have wrestled for ye with the Lord!" Here the loud tones of his voice sank into tenderness.

"And her too, poor woman! poor woman! her you are calling upon. She's not here. You'll find her with the Lord. Go there and seek her, not here. Do you hear me, lad? go after her there. He'll let you in, though it's late. Man, take heart! if you will lie and sob and greet, let it be at heaven's gate, and not your poor mother's ruined door."

He stopped to get his breath; and the voice had stopped, not as it had done before, when its time was exhausted and all its repetitions said, but with a sobbing catch in the breath as if overruled. Then the minister spoke again, "Are you hearing me, Will? Oh, laddie, you've liked the beggarly elements all your days. Be done with them now. Go home to the Father—the Father! Are you hearing me?" Here the old man sank down upon his knees, his face raised upwards, his hands held up with a tremble in them, all white in the light in the midst of the darkness. I resisted as long as I could, though I cannot tell why; then I, too, dropped upon my knees. Simson all the time stood in the door-way, with an expression in his face such as words could not tell, his under lip dropped, his eyes wild, staring. It seemed to be to him, that image of blank ignorance and wonder, that we were praying. All the time the voice, with a low arrested sobbing, lay just where he was standing, as I thought.

"Lord," the minister said,—"Lord, take him into Thy everlasting habitations. The mother he cries to is with Thee. Who can open to him but Thee? Lord, when is it too late for Thee, or what is too hard for Thee? Lord, let that woman there draw him inower! Let her draw him inower!"

I sprang forward to catch something in my arms that flung itself wildly within the door. The illusion was so strong, that I never paused till I felt my forehead graze against the wall and my hands clutch the ground,—for there was nobody there to save from falling, as in my foolishness I thought. Simson held out his hand to me to help me up. He was trembling and cold, his lower lip hanging, his speech almost inarticulate. "It's gone," he said, stammering,—"it's gone!" We leaned upon each other for a moment, trembling so much, both of us, that the whole scene trembled as if it were going to dissolve and disappear; and yet as long as I live I will never forget it,—the shining of the strange lights, the blackness all round, the kneeling figure with all the whiteness of the light concentrated on its white venerable head and uplifted hands. A strange solemn stillness seemed to close all round us. By intervals a single syllable, "Lord! Lord!" came from the old minister's lips. He saw none of us, nor thought of us. I never knew how long we stood, like sentinels guarding him at his prayers, holding our lights in a confused dazed way, not knowing what we did. But at last he rose from his knees, and standing up at his full height, raised his arms, as the Scotch manner is at the end of a religious service, and solemnly gave the apostolical benediction,—to what? to the silent earth, the dark woods, the wide breathing atmosphere; for we were but spectators gasping an Amen!

It seemed to me that it must be the middle of the night, as we all walked back. It was in reality very late. Dr. Moncrieff put his arm into mine. He walked slowly, with an air of exhaustion. It was as if we were coming from a death-bed. Something hushed and solemnized the very air. There was that sense of relief in it which there always is at the end of a death-struggle. And nature, persistent, never daunted, came back in all of us, as we returned into the ways of life. We said nothing to each other, indeed, for a time; but when we got clear of the trees and reached the opening near the house, where we could see the sky, Dr. Moncrieff himself was the first to speak. "I must be going," he said; "it's very late, I'm afraid. I will go down the glen, as I came."

"But not alone. I am going with you, Doctor."

"Well, I will not oppose it. I am an old man, and agitation wearies more than work. Yes; I'll be thankful of your arm. To-night, Colonel, you've done me more good turns than one."

I pressed his hand on my arm, not feeling able to speak. But Simson, who turned with us, and who had gone along all this time with his taper flaring, in entire unconsciousness, came to himself, apparently at the sound of our voices, and put out that wild little torch with a quick movement, as if of shame. "Let me carry your lantern," he said; "it is heavy." He recovered with a spring; and in a moment, from the awe-stricken spectator he had been, became himself, sceptical and cynical. "I should like to ask you a question," he said. "Do you believe in Purgatory, Doctor? It's not in the tenets of the Church, so far as I know."

"Sir," said Dr. Moncrieff, "an old man like me is sometimes not very sure what he believes. There is just one thing I am certain of—and that is the loving-kindness of God."

"But I thought that was in this life. I am no theologian—"

"Sir," said the old man again, with a tremor in him which I could feel going over all his frame, "if I saw a friend of mine within the gates of hell, I would not despair but his Father would take him by the hand still, if he cried like you."

"I allow it is very strange, very strange. I cannot see through it. That there must be human agency, I feel sure. Doctor, what made you decide upon the person and the name?"

The minister put out his hand with the impatience which a man might show if he were asked how he recognized his brother. "Tuts!" he said, in familiar speech; then more solemnly, "How should I not recognize a person that I know better—far better—than I know you?"

"Then you saw the man?"

Dr. Moncrieff made no reply. He moved his hand again with a little impatient movement, and walked on, leaning heavily on my arm. And we went on for a long time without another word, threading the dark paths, which were steep and slippery with the damp of the winter. The air was very still,—not more than enough to make a faint sighing in the branches, which mingled with the sound of the water to which we were descending. When we spoke again, it was about indifferent matters,—about the height of the river, and the recent rains. We parted with the minister at his own door, where his old housekeeper appeared in great perturbation, waiting for him. "Eh, me, minister! the young gentleman will be worse?" she cried.

"Far from that—better. God bless him!" Dr. Moncrieff said.

I think if Simson had begun again to me with his questions, I should have pitched him over the rocks as we returned up the glen; but he was silent, by a good inspiration. And the sky was clearer than it had been for many nights, shining high over the trees, with here and there a star faintly gleaming through the wilderness of dark and bare branches. The air, as I have said, was very soft in them, with a subdued and peaceful cadence. It was real, like every natural sound, and came to us like a hush of peace and relief. I thought there was a sound in it as of the breath of a sleeper, and it seemed clear to me that Roland must be sleeping, satisfied and calm. We went up to his room when we went in. There we found the complete hush of rest. My wife looked up out of a doze, and gave me a smile: "I think he is a great deal better; but you are very late," she said in a whisper, shading the light with her hand that the Doctor might see his patient. The boy had got back something like his own color. He woke as we stood all round his bed. His eyes had the happy, half-awakened look of childhood, glad to shut again, yet pleased with the interruption and glimmer of the light. I stooped over him and kissed his forehead, which was moist and cool. "All is well, Roland," I said. He looked up at me with a glance of pleasure, and took my hand and laid his cheek upon it, and so went to sleep.

For some nights after, I watched among the ruins, spending all the dark hours up to midnight patrolling about the bit of wall which was associated with so many emotions; but I heard nothing, and saw nothing beyond the quiet course of nature; nor, so far as I am aware, has anything been heard again. Dr. Moncrieff gave me the history of the youth, whom he never hesitated to name. I did not ask, as Simson did, how he recognized him. He had been a prodigal,—weak, foolish, easily imposed upon, and "led away," as people say. All that we had heard had passed actually in life, the Doctor said. The young man had come home thus a day or two after his mother died,—who was no more than the housekeeper in the old house,—and distracted with the news, had thrown himself down at the door and called upon her to let him in. The old man could scarcely speak of it for tears. To me it seemed as if—Heaven help us, how little do we know about anything!—a scene like that might impress itself somehow upon the hidden heart of nature. I do not pretend to know how, but the repetition had struck me at the time as, in its terrible strangeness and incomprehensibility, almost mechanical,—as if the unseen actor could not exceed or vary, but was bound to re-enact the whole. One thing that struck me, however, greatly, was the likeness between the old minister and my boy in the manner of regarding these strange phenomena. Dr. Moncrieff was not terrified, as I had been myself, and all the rest of us. It was no "ghost," as I fear we all vulgarly considered it, to him,—but a poor creature whom he knew under these conditions, just as he had known him in the flesh, having no doubt of his identity. And to Roland it was the same. This spirit in pain,—if it was a spirit,—this voice out of the unseen,—was a poor fellow-creature in misery, to be succored and helped out of his trouble, to my boy. He spoke to me quite frankly about it when he got better. "I knew father would find out some way," he said. And this was when he was strong and well, and all idea that he would turn hysterical or become a seer of visions had happily passed away.

I must add one curious fact, which does not seem to me to have any relation to the above, but which Simson made great use of, as the human agency which he was determined to find somehow. We had examined the ruins very closely at the time of these occurrences; but afterwards, when all was over, as we went casually about them one Sunday afternoon in the idleness of that unemployed day, Simson with his stick penetrated an old window which had been entirely blocked up with fallen soil. He jumped down into it in great excitement, and called me to follow. There we found a little hole,—for it was more a hole than a room,—entirely hidden under the ivy and ruins, in which there was a quantity of straw laid in a corner, as if some one had made a bed there, and some remains of crusts about the floor. Some one had lodged there, and not very long before, he made out; and that this unknown being was the author of all the mysterious sounds we heard he is convinced. "I told you it was human agency," he said triumphantly. He forgets, I suppose, how he and I stood with our lights, seeing nothing, while the space between us was audibly traversed by something that could speak, and sob, and suffer. There is no argument with men of this kind. He is ready to get up a laugh against me on this slender ground. "I was puzzled myself,—I could not make it out,—but I always felt convinced human agency was at the bottom of it. And here it is,—and a clever fellow he must have been," the Doctor says.

Bagley left my service as soon as he got well. He assured me it was no want of respect, but he could not stand "them kind of things;" and the man was so shaken and ghastly that I was glad to give him a present and let him go. For my own part, I made a point of staying out the time—two years—for which I had taken Brentwood; but I did not renew my tenancy. By that time we had settled, and found for ourselves a pleasant home of our own.

I must add, that when the Doctor defies me, I can always bring back gravity to his countenance, and a pause in his railing, when I remind him of the juniper-bush. To me that was a matter of little importance. I could believe I was mistaken. I did not care about it one way or other; but on his mind the effect was different. The miserable voice, the spirit in pain, he could think of as the result of ventriloquism, or reverberation, or—anything you please: an elaborate prolonged hoax, executed somehow by the tramp that had found a lodging in the old tower; but the juniper-bush staggered him. Things have effects so different on the minds of different men.

II

THE PORTRAIT

At the period when the following incidents occurred, I was living with my father at The Grove, a large old house in the immediate neighborhood of a little town. This had been his home for a number of years; and I believe I was born in it. It was a kind of house which, notwithstanding all the red and white architecture known at present by the name of Queen Anne, builders nowadays have forgotten how to build. It was straggling and irregular, with wide passages, wide staircases, broad landings; the rooms large but not very lofty; the arrangements leaving much to be desired, with no economy of space; a house belonging to a period when land was cheap, and, so far as that was concerned, there was no occasion to economize. Though it was so near the town, the clump of trees in which it was environed was a veritable grove. In the grounds in spring the primroses grew as thickly as in the forest. We had a few fields for the cows, and an excellent walled garden. The place is being pulled down at this moment to make room for more streets of mean little houses,—the kind of thing, and not a dull house of faded gentry, which perhaps the neighborhood requires. The house was dull, and so were we, its last inhabitants; and the furniture was faded, even a little dingy,—nothing to brag of. I do not, however, intend to convey a suggestion that we were faded gentry, for that was not the case. My father, indeed, was rich, and had no need to spare any expense in making his life and his house bright if he pleased; but he did not please, and I had not been long enough at home to exercise any special influence of my own. It was the only home I had ever known; but except in my earliest childhood, and in my holidays as a schoolboy, I had in reality known but little of it. My mother had died at my birth, or shortly after, and I had grown up in the gravity and silence of a house without women. In my infancy, I believe, a sister of my father's had lived with us, and taken charge of the household and of me; but she, too, had died long, long ago, my mourning for her being one of the first things I could recollect. And she had no successor. There were, indeed, a housekeeper and some maids,—the latter of whom I only saw disappearing at the end of a passage, or whisking out of a room when one of "the gentlemen" appeared. Mrs. Weir, indeed, I saw nearly every day; but a curtsey, a smile, a pair of nice round arms which she caressed while folding them across her ample waist, and a large white apron, were all I knew of her. This was the only female influence in the house. The drawing-room I was aware of only as a place of deadly good order, into which nobody ever entered. It had three long windows opening on the lawn, and communicated at the upper end, which was rounded like a great bay, with the conservatory. Sometimes I gazed into it as a child from without, wondering at the needlework on the chairs, the screens, the looking-glasses which never reflected any living face. My father did not like the room, which probably was not wonderful, though it never occurred to me in those early days to inquire why.

I may say here, though it will probably be disappointing to those who form a sentimental idea of the capabilities of children, that it did not occur to me either, in these early days, to make any inquiry about my mother. There was no room in life, as I knew it, for any such person; nothing suggested to my mind either the fact that she must have existed, or that there was need of her in the house. I accepted, as I believe most children do, the facts of existence, on the basis with which I had first made acquaintance with them, without question or remark. As a matter of fact, I was aware that it was rather dull at home; but neither by comparison with the books I read, nor by the communications received from my school-fellows, did this seem to me anything remarkable. And I was possibly somewhat dull too by nature, for I did not mind. I was fond of reading, and for that there was unbounded opportunity. I had a little ambition in respect to work, and that too could be prosecuted undisturbed. When I went to the university, my society lay almost entirely among men; but by that time and afterwards, matters had of course greatly changed with me, and though I recognized women as part of the economy of nature, and did not indeed by any means dislike or avoid them, yet the idea of connecting them at all with my own home never entered into my head. That continued to be as it had always been, when at intervals I descended upon the cool, grave, colorless place, in the midst of my traffic with the world: always very still, well-ordered, serious,—the cooking very good, the comfort perfect; old Morphew, the butler, a little older (but very little older, perhaps on the whole less old, since in my childhood I had thought him a kind of Methuselah); and Mrs. Weir, less active, covering up her arms in sleeves, but folding and caressing them just as always. I remember looking in from the lawn through the windows upon that deadly-orderly drawing-room, with a humorous recollection of my childish admiration and wonder, and feeling that it must be kept so forever and ever, and that to go into it would break some sort of amusing mock mystery, some pleasantly ridiculous spell.

But it was only at rare intervals that I went home. In the long vacation, as in my school holidays, my father often went abroad with me, so that we had gone over a great deal of the Continent together very pleasantly. He was old in proportion to the age of his son, being a man of sixty when I was twenty, but that did not disturb the pleasure of the relations between us. I don't know that they were ever very confidential. On my side there was but little to communicate, for I did not get into scrapes nor fall in love, the two predicaments which demand sympathy and confidences. And as for my father himself, I was never aware what there could be to communicate on his side. I knew his life exactly,—what he did almost at every hour of the day; under what circumstances of the temperature he would ride and when walk; how often and with what guests he would indulge in the occasional break of a dinner-party, a serious pleasure,—perhaps, indeed, less a pleasure than a duty. All this I knew as well as he did, and also his views on public matters, his political opinions, which naturally were different from mine. What ground, then, remained for confidence? I did not know any. We were both of us of a reserved nature, not apt to enter into our religious feelings, for instance. There are many people who think reticence on such subjects a sign of the most reverential way of contemplating them. Of this I am far from being sure; but, at all events, it was the practice most congenial to my own mind.

And then I was for a long time absent, making my own way in the world. I did not make it very successfully. I accomplished the natural fate of an Englishman, and went out to the Colonies;

then to India in a semi-diplomatic position; but returned home after seven or eight years, invalided, in bad health and not much better spirits, tired and disappointed with my first trial of life. I had, as people say, "no occasion" to insist on making my way. My father was rich, and had never given me the slightest reason to believe that he did not intend me to be his heir. His allowance to me was not illiberal, and though he did not oppose the carrying out of my own plans, he by no means urged me to exertion. When I came home he received me very affectionately, and expressed his satisfaction in my return. "Of course," he said, "I am not glad that you are disappointed, Philip, or that your health is broken; but otherwise it is an ill wind, you know, that blows nobody good; and I am very glad to have you at home. I am growing an old man—"

"I don't see any difference, sir," said I; "everything here seems exactly the same as when I went away—"

He smiled, and shook his head. "It is true enough," he said; "after we have reached a certain age we seem to go on for a long time on a plane, and feel no great difference from year to year; but it is an inclined plane, and the longer we go on the more sudden will be the fall at the end. But at all events it will be a great comfort to me to have you here."

"If I had known that," I said, "and that you wanted me, I should have come in any circumstances. As there are only two of us in the world—"

"Yes," he said, "there are only two of us in the world; but still I should not have sent for you, Phil, to interrupt your career."

"It is as well, then, that it has interrupted itself," I said rather bitterly; for disappointment is hard to bear.

He patted me on the shoulder, and repeated, "It is an ill wind that blows nobody good," with a look of real pleasure which gave me a certain gratification too; for, after all, he was an old man, and the only one in all the world to whom I owed any duty. I had not been without dreams of warmer affections, but they had come to nothing—not tragically, but in the ordinary way. I might perhaps have had love which I did not want but not that which I did want,—which was not a thing to make any unmanly moan about, but in the ordinary course of events. Such disappointments happen every day; indeed, they are more common than anything else, and sometimes it is apparent afterwards that it is better it was so.

However, here I was at thirty stranded, yet wanting for nothing,—in a position to call forth rather envy than pity from the greater part of my contemporaries; for I had an assured and comfortable existence, as much money as I wanted, and the prospect of an excellent fortune for the future. On the other hand, my health was still low, and I had no occupation. The neighborhood of the town was a drawback rather than an advantage. I felt myself tempted, instead of taking the long walk into the country which my doctor recommended, to take a much shorter one through the High Street, across the river, and back again, which was not a walk but a lounge. The country was silent and full of thoughts,—thoughts not always very agreeable,—whereas there were always the humors of the little urban population to glance at, the news to be heard,—all those petty matters which so often make up life in a very impoverished version for the idle man. I did not like it, but I felt myself yielding to it, not having energy enough to make a stand. The rector and the leading lawyer of the place asked me to dinner. I might have glided into the society, such as it was, had I been disposed for that; everything about me began to close over me as if I had been fifty, and fully contented with my lot.

It was possibly my own want of occupation which made me observe with surprise, after a while, how much occupied my father was. He had expressed himself glad of my return; but now that I had returned, I saw very little of him. Most of his time was spent in his library, as had always been the case. But on the few visits I paid him there, I could not but perceive that the aspect of the library was much changed. It had acquired the look of a business-room, almost an office. There were large business-like books on the table, which I could not associate with anything he could naturally have to do; and his correspondence was very large. I thought he closed one of those books hurriedly as I came in, and pushed it away, as if he did not wish me to see it. This surprised me at the moment without arousing any other feeling; but afterwards I remembered it with a clearer sense of what it meant. He was more absorbed altogether than I had been used to see him. He was visited by men sometimes not of very prepossessing appearance. Surprise grew in my mind without any very distinct idea of the reason of it; and it was not till after a chance conversation with Morphew that my vague uneasiness began to take definite shape. It was begun without any special intention on my part. Morphew had informed me that master was very busy, on some occasion when I wanted to see him. And I was a little annoyed to be thus put off. "It appears to me that my father is always busy," I said hastily. Morphew then began very oracularly to nod his head in assent.

"A deal too busy, sir, if you take my opinion," he said.

This startled me much, and I asked hurriedly, "What do you mean?" without reflecting that to ask for private information from a servant about my father's habits was as bad as investigating into a stranger's affairs. It did not strike me in the same light.

"Mr. Philip," said Morphew, "a thing 'as 'appened as 'appens more often than it ought to. Master has got awful keen about money in his old age."

"That's a new thing for him," I said.

"No, sir, begging your pardon, it ain't a new thing. He was once broke of it, and that wasn't easy done; but it's come back, if you'll excuse me saying so. And I don't know as he'll ever be broke of it again at his age."

I felt more disposed to be angry than disturbed by this. "You must be making some ridiculous mistake," I said. "And if you were not so old a friend as you are, Morphew, I should not have allowed my father to be so spoken of to me."

The old man gave me a half-astonished, half-contemptuous look. "He's been my master a deal longer than he's been your father," he said, turning on his heel. The assumption was so comical that my anger could not stand in face of it. I went out, having been on my way to the door when this conversation occurred, and took my usual lounge about, which was not a satisfactory sort of amusement. Its vanity and emptiness appeared to be more evident than usual to-day. I met half-a-dozen people I knew, and had as many pieces of news confided to me. I went up and down the length of the High Street. I made a small purchase or two. And then I turned homeward, despising myself, yet finding no alternative within my reach. Would a long country walk have been more virtuous? It would at least have been more wholesome; but that was all that could be said. My mind did not dwell on Morphew's communication. It seemed without sense or meaning to me; and after the excellent joke about his superior interest in his master to mine in my father, was dismissed lightly enough from my mind. I tried to invent some way of telling this to my father without letting him perceive that Morphew had been finding faults in him, or I listening; for it seemed a pity to lose so good a joke. However, as I returned home, something happened which put the joke entirely out of my head. It is curious when a new subject of trouble or anxiety has been suggested to the mind in an unexpected way, how often a second advertisement follows immediately after the first, and gives to that a potency which in itself it had not possessed.

I was approaching our own door, wondering whether my father had gone, and whether, on my return, I should find him at leisure,—for I had several little things to say to him,—when I noticed a poor woman lingering about the closed gates. She had a baby sleeping in her arms. It was a spring night, the stars shining in the twilight, and everything soft and dim; and the woman's figure was like a shadow, flitting about, now here, now there, on one side or another of the gate. She stopped when she saw me approaching, and hesitated for a moment, then seemed to take a sudden resolution. I watched her without knowing, with a prevision that she was going to address me, though with no sort of idea as to the subject of her address. She came up to me doubtfully, it seemed, yet certainly, as I felt, and when she was close to me, dropped a sort of hesitating curtsey, and said, "It's Mr. Philip?" in a low voice.

"What do you want with me?" I said.

Then she poured forth suddenly, without warning or preparation, her long speech,—a flood of words which must have been all ready and waiting at the doors of her lips for utterance. "Oh, sir, I want to speak to you! I can't believe you'll be so hard, for you're young; and I can't believe he'll be so hard if so be as his own son, as I've always heard he had but one, 'll speak up for us. Oh, gentleman, it is easy for the likes of you, that, if you ain't comfortable in one room, can just walk into another; but if one room is all you have, and every bit of furniture you have taken out of it, and nothing but the four walls left,—not so much as the cradle for the child, or a chair for your man to sit down upon when he comes from his work, or a saucepan to cook him his supper—"

"My good woman," I said, "who can have taken all that from you? Surely nobody can be so cruel?"

"You say it's cruel!" she cried with a sort of triumph. "Oh, I knowed you would, or any true gentleman that don't hold with screwing poor folks. Just go and say that to him inside there for the love of God. Tell him to think what he's doing, driving poor creatures to despair. Summer's coming, the Lord be praised, but yet it's bitter cold at night with your counterpane gone; and when you've been working hard all day, and nothing but four bare walls to come home to, and all your poor little sticks of furniture that you've saved up for, and got together one by one, all gone, and you no better than when you started, or rather worse, for then you was young. Oh, sir!" the woman's voice rose into a sort of passionate wail. And then she added, beseechingly, recovering herself, "Oh, speak for us; he'll not refuse his own son—"

"To whom am I to speak? Who is it that has done this to you?" I said.

The woman hesitated again, looking keenly in my face, then repeated with a slight faltering, "It's Mr. Philip?" as if that made everything right.

"Yes; I am Philip Canning," I said; "but what have I to do with this? and to whom am I to speak?"

She began to whimper, crying and stopping herself. "Oh, please, sir! it's Mr. Canning as owns all the house property about; it's him that our court and the lane and everything belongs to. And he's taken the bed from under us, and the baby's cradle, although it's said in the Bible as you're not to take poor folks' bed."

"My father!" I cried in spite of myself; "then it must be some agent, some one else in his name. You may be sure he knows nothing of it. Of course I shall speak to him at once."

"Oh, God bless you, sir," said the woman. But then she added, in a lower tone, "It's no agent. It's one as never knows trouble. It's him that lives in that grand house." But this was said under her breath, evidently not for me to hear.

Morphew's words flashed through my mind as she spoke. What was this? Did it afford an explanation of the much-occupied hours, the big books, the strange visitors? I took the poor woman's name, and gave her something to procure a few comforts for the night, and went indoors disturbed and troubled. It was impossible to believe that my father himself would have acted thus; but he was not a man to brook interference, and I did not see how to introduce the subject, what to say. I could but hope that, at the moment of broaching it, words would be put into my mouth, which often happens in moments of necessity, one knows not how, even when one's theme is not so all-important as that for which such help has been promised. As usual, I did not see my father till dinner. I have said that our dinners were very good, luxurious in a simple way, everything excellent in its kind, well cooked, well served,—the perfection of comfort without show,—which is a combination very dear to the English heart. I said nothing till Morphew, with his solemn attention to everything that was going, had retired; and then it was with some strain of courage that I began.

"I was stopped outside the gate to-day by a curious sort of petitioner,—a poor woman, who seems to be one of your tenants, sir, but whom your agent must have been rather too hard upon."

"My agent? Who is that?" said my father quietly.

"I don't know his name, and I doubt his competence. The poor creature seems to have had everything taken from her,—her bed, her child's cradle."

"No doubt she was behind with her rent."

"Very likely, sir. She seemed very poor," said I.

"You take it coolly," said my father, with an upward glance, half-amused, not in the least shocked by my statement. "But when a man, or a woman either, takes a house, I suppose you will allow that they ought to pay rent for it."

"Certainly, sir," I replied, "when they have got anything to pay."

"I don't allow the reservation," he said. But he was not angry, which I had feared he would be.

"I think," I continued, "that your agent must be too severe. And this emboldens me to say something which has been in my mind for some time"—(these were the words, no doubt, which I had hoped would be put into my month; they were the suggestion of the moment, and yet as I said them it was with the most complete conviction of their truth)—"and that is this: I am doing nothing; my time hangs heavy on my hands. Make me your agent. I will see for myself, and save you from such mistakes; and it will be an occupation—"

"Mistakes? What warrant have you for saying these are mistakes?" he said testily; then after a moment: "This is a strange proposal from you, Phil. Do you know what it is you are offering?—to be a collector of rents, going about from door to door, from week to week; to look after wretched little bits of repairs, drains, etc.; to get paid, which, after all, is the chief thing, and not to be taken in by tales of poverty."

"Not to let you be taken in by men without pity," I said.

He gave me a strange glance, which I did not very well understand, and said abruptly, a thing which, so far as I remember, he had never in my life said before, "You've become a little like your mother, Phil—"

"My mother!" the reference was so unusual—nay, so unprecedented—that I was greatly startled. It seemed to me like the sudden introduction of a quite new element in the stagnant atmosphere, as well as a new party to our conversation. My father looked across the table, as if with some astonishment at my tone of surprise.

"Is that so very extraordinary?" he said.

"No; of course it is not extraordinary that I should resemble my mother. Only—I have heard very little of her—almost nothing."

"That is true." He got up and placed himself before the fire, which was very low, as the night was not cold—had not been cold heretofore at least; but it seemed to me now that a little chill came into the dim and faded room. Perhaps it looked more dull from the suggestion of a something brighter, warmer, that might have been. "Talking of mistakes," he said, "perhaps that was one: to sever you entirely from her side of the house. But I did not care for the connection. You will understand how it is that I speak of it now when I tell you—" He stopped here, however, said nothing more for a minute or so, and then rang the bell. Morphew came, as he always did, very deliberately, so that some time elapsed in silence, during which my surprise grew. When the old man appeared at the door—"Have you put the lights in the drawing-room, as I told you?" my father said.

"Yes, sir; and opened the box, sir; and it's a—it's a speaking likeness—"

This the old man got out in a great hurry, as if afraid that his master would stop him. My father did so with a wave of his hand.

"That's enough. I asked no information. You can go now."

The door closed upon us, and there was again a pause. My subject had floated away altogether like a mist, though I had been so concerned about it. I tried to resume, but could not. Something seemed to arrest my very breathing; and yet in this dull, respectable house of ours, where everything breathed good character and integrity, it was certain that there could be no shameful mystery to reveal. It was some time before my father spoke, not from any purpose that I could see, but apparently because his mind was busy with probably unaccustomed thoughts.

"You scarcely know the drawing-room, Phil," he said at last.

"Very little. I have never seen it used. I have a little awe of it, to tell the truth."

"That should not be. There is no reason for that. But a man by himself, as I have been for the greater part of my life, has no occasion for a drawing-room. I always, as a matter of preference, sat among my books; however, I ought to have thought of the impression on you."

"Oh, it is not important," I said; "the awe was childish. I have not thought of it since I came home."

"It never was anything very splendid at the best," said he. He lifted the lamp from the table with a sort of abstraction, not remarking even my offer to take it from him, and led the way. He was on the verge of seventy, and looked his age; but it was a vigorous age, with no symptom of giving way. The circle of light from the lamp lit up his white hair and keen blue eyes and clear complexion; his forehead was like old ivory, his cheek warmly colored; an old man, yet a man in full strength. He was taller than I was, and still almost as strong. As he stood for a moment with the lamp in his hand, he looked like a tower in his great height and bulk. I reflected as I looked at him that I knew him intimately, more intimately than any other creature in the world,—I was familiar with every detail of his outward life; could it be that in reality I did not know him at all?

The drawing-room was already lighted with a flickering array of candles upon the mantelpiece and along the walls, producing the pretty, starry effect which candles give without very much light. As I had not the smallest idea what I was about to see, for Morphew's "speaking likeness" was very hurriedly said, and only half comprehensible in the bewilderment of my faculties, my first glance was at this very unusual illumination, for which I could assign no reason. The next showed me a large full-length portrait, still in the box in which apparently it had travelled, placed upright, supported against a table in the centre of the room. My father walked straight up to it, motioned to me to place a smaller table close to the picture on the left side, and put his lamp upon that. Then he waved his hand towards it, and stood aside that I might see.

It was a full-length portrait of a very young woman—I might say a girl scarcely twenty—in a white dress, made in a very simple old fashion, though I was too little accustomed to female costume to be able to fix the date. It might have been a hundred years old, or twenty, for aught I knew. The face had an expression of youth, candor, and simplicity more than any face I had ever seen,—or so, at least in my surprise, I thought. The eyes were a little wistful, with something which was almost anxiety which at least was not content—in them; a faint, almost imperceptible, curve in the lids. The complexion was of a dazzling fairness, the hair light, but the eyes dark, which gave individuality to the face. It would have been as lovely had the eyes been blue,—probably more so,—but their darkness gave a touch of character, a slight discord, which made the harmony finer. It was not, perhaps, beautiful in the highest sense of the word. The girl must have been too young, too slight, too little developed for actual beauty; but a face which so invited love and confidence I never saw. One smiled at it with instinctive affection. "What a sweet face!" I said. "What a lovely girl! Who is she? Is this one of the relations you were speaking of on the other side?"

My father made me no reply. He stood aside, looking at it as if he knew it too well to require to look,—as if the picture was already in his eyes. "Yes," he said, after an interval, with a long-drawn breath, "she was a lovely girl, as you say."

"Was?—then she is dead. What a pity!" I said; "what a pity! so young and so sweet!"

We stood gazing at her thus, in her beautiful stillness and calm,—two men, the younger of us full-grown and conscious of many experiences, the other an old man,—before this impersonation of tender youth. At length he said, with a slight tremulousness in his voice, "Does nothing suggest to you who she is, Phil?"

I turned round to look at him with profound astonishment, but he turned away from my look. A sort of quiver passed over his face. "That is your mother," he said, and walked suddenly away, leaving me there.

My mother!

I stood for a moment in a kind of consternation before the white-robed innocent creature, to me no more than a child; then a sudden laugh broke from me, without any will of mine something ludicrous, as well as something awful, was in it. When the laugh was over, I found myself with tears in my eyes, gazing, holding my breath. The soft features seemed to melt, the lips to move, the anxiety in the eyes to become a personal inquiry. Ah, no! nothing of the kind; only because of the water in mine. My mother! oh, fair and gentle creature, scarcely woman, how could any man's voice call her by that name! I had little idea enough of what it meant,—had heard it laughed at, scoffed at, reverenced, but never had learned to place it even among the ideal powers of life. Yet if it meant anything at all, what it meant was worth thinking of. What did she ask, looking at me with those eyes? What would she have said if "those lips had language"? If I had known her only as Cowper did—with a child's recollection—there might have been some thread, some faint but comprehensible link, between us; but now all that I felt was the curious incongruity. Poor child! I said to myself; so sweet a creature: poor little tender soul! as if she had been a little sister, a child of mine,—but my mother! I cannot tell how long I stood looking at her, studying the candid, sweet face, which surely had germs in it of everything that was good and beautiful; and sorry, with a profound regret, that she had died and never carried these promises to fulfillment. Poor girl! poor people who had loved her! These were my thoughts; with a curious vertigo and giddiness of my whole being in the sense of a mysterious relationship, which it was beyond my power to understand.

Presently my father came back, possibly because I had been a long time unconscious of the passage of the minutes, or perhaps because he was himself restless in the strange disturbance of his habitual calm. He came in and put his arm within mine, leaning his weight partially upon me, with an affectionate suggestion which went deeper than words. I pressed his arm to my side: it was more between us two grave Englishmen than any embracing.

"I cannot understand it," I said.

"No. I don't wonder at that; but if it is strange to you, Phil, think how much more strange to me! That is the partner of my life. I have never had another, or thought of another. That—girl! If we are to meet again, as I have always hoped we should meet again, what am I to say to her,—I, an old man? Yes; I know what you mean. I am not an old man for my years; but my years are threescore and ten, and the play is nearly played out. How am I to meet that young creature? We used to say to each other that it was forever, that we never could be but one, that it was for life and death. But what—what am I to say to her, Phil, when I meet her again, that—that angel? No, it is not her being an angel that troubles me; but she is so young! She is like my—my granddaughter," he cried, with a burst of what was half sobs, half laughter; "and she is my wife,—and I am an old man—an old man! And so much has happened that she could not understand."

I was too much startled by this strange complaint to know what to say. It was not my own trouble, and I answered it in the conventional way.

"They are not as we are, sir," I said; "they look upon us with larger, other eyes than ours."

"Ah! you don't know what I mean," he said quickly; and in the interval he had subdued his emotion. "At first, after she died, it was my consolation to think that I should meet her again,—that we never could be really parted. But, my God, how I have changed since then! I am another man,—I am a different being. I was not very young even then,—twenty years older than she was; but her youth renewed mine. I was not an unfit partner; she asked no better, and knew as much more than I did in some things,—being so much nearer the source,—as I did in others that were of the world. But I have gone a long way since then, Phil,—a long way; and there she stands, just where I left her."

I pressed his arm again. "Father," I said, which was a title I seldom used, "we are not to suppose that in a higher life the mind stands still." I did not feel myself qualified to discuss such topics, but something one must say.

"Worse, worse!" he replied; "then she too will be, like me, a different being, and we shall meet as what? as strangers, as people who have lost sight of each other, with a long past between us,—we who parted, my God! with—with—"

His voice broke and ended for a moment then while, surprised and almost shocked by what he said, I cast about in my mind what to reply, he withdrew his arm suddenly from mine, and said in his usual tone, "Where shall we hang the picture, Phil? It must be here in this room. What do you think will be the best light?"

This sudden alteration took me still more by surprise, and gave me almost an additional shock; but it was evident that I must follow the changes of his mood, or at least the sudden repression of sentiment which he originated. We went into that simpler question with great seriousness, consulting which would be the best light. "You know I can scarcely advise," I said; "I have never been familiar with this room. I should like to put off, if you don't mind, till daylight."

"I think," he said, "that this would be the best place." It was on the other side of the fireplace, on the wall which faced the windows,—not the best light, I knew enough to be aware, for an oil-painting. When I said so, however, he answered me with a little impatience, "It does not matter very much about the best light; there will be nobody to see it but you and me. I have my reasons—" There was a small table standing against the wall at this spot, on which he had his hand as he spoke. Upon it stood a little basket in very fine lace-like wicker-work. His hand must have trembled, for the table shook, and the basket fell, its contents turning out upon the carpet,—little bits of needlework, colored silks, a small piece of knitting half done. He laughed as they rolled out at his feet, and tried to stoop to collect them, then tottered to a chair, and covered for a moment his face with his hands.

No need to ask what they were. No woman's work had been seen in the house since I could recollect it. I gathered them up reverently and put them back. I could see, ignorant as I was, that the bit of knitting was something for an infant. What could I do less than put it to my lips? It had been left in the doing—for me.

"Yes, I think this is the best place," my father said a minute after, in his usual tone.

We placed it there that evening with our own hands. The picture was large, and in a heavy frame, but my father would let no one help me but himself. And then, with a superstition for which I never could give any reason even to myself, having removed the packings, we closed and locked the door, leaving the candles about the room, in their soft, strange illumination, lighting the first night of her return to her old place.

That night no more was said. My father went to his room early, which was not his habit. He had never, however, accustomed me to sit late with him in the library. I had a little study or smoking-room of my own, in which all my special treasures were, the collections of my travels and my favorite books,—and where I always sat after prayers, a ceremonial which was regularly kept up in the house. I retired as usual this night to my room, and, as usual, read,—but to-night somewhat vaguely, often pausing to think. When it was quite late, I went out by the glass door to the lawn, and walked round the house, with the intention of looking in at the drawing-room windows, as I had done when a child. But I had forgotten that these windows were all shuttered at night; and nothing but a faint penetration of the light within through the crevices bore witness to the installment of the new dweller there.

In the morning my father was entirely himself again. He told me without emotion of the manner in which he had obtained the picture. It had belonged to my mother's family, and had fallen eventually into the hands of a cousin of hers, resident abroad,— "A man whom I did not like, and who did not like me," my father said; "there was, or had been, some rivalry, he thought: a mistake, but he was never aware of that. He refused all my requests to have a copy made. You may suppose, Phil, that I wished this very much. Had I succeeded, you would have been acquainted, at least, with your mother's appearance, and need not have sustained this shock. But he would not consent. It gave him, I think, a certain pleasure to think that he had the only picture. But now he is dead, and out of remorse, or with some other intention, has left it to me."

"That looks like kindness," said I.

"Yes; or something else. He might have thought that by so doing he was establishing a claim upon me," my father said; but he did not seem disposed to add any more. On whose behalf he meant to establish a claim I did not know, nor who the man was who had laid us under so great an obligation on his death-bed. He had established a claim on me at least; though, as he was dead, I could not see on whose behalf it was. And my father said nothing more; he seemed to dislike the subject. When I attempted to return to it, he had recourse to his letters or his newspapers. Evidently he had made up his mind to say no more.

Afterwards I went into the drawing-room, to look at the picture once more. It seemed to me that the anxiety in her eyes was not so evident as I had thought it last night. The light possibly was more favorable. She stood just above the place where, I make no doubt, she had sat in life, where her little work-basket was,—not very much above it. The picture was full-length, and we had hung it low, so that she might have been stepping into the room, and was little above my own level as I stood and looked at her again. Once more I smiled at the strange thought that this young creature—so young, almost childish—could be my mother; and once more my eyes grew wet looking at her. He was a benefactor, indeed, who had given her back to us. I said to myself, that if I could ever do anything for him or his, I would certainly do it, for my—for this lovely young creature's sake. And with this in my mind, and all the thoughts that came with it, I am obliged to confess that the other matter, which I had been so full of on the previous night, went entirely out of my head.

It is rarely, however, that such matters are allowed to slip out of one's mind. When I went out in the afternoon for my usual stroll,—or rather when I returned from that stroll,—I saw once more before me the woman with her baby, whose story had filled me with dismay on the previous evening. She was waiting at the gate as before, and, "Oh, gentleman, but haven't you got some news to give me?" she said.

"My good woman,—I—have been greatly occupied. I have had—no time to do anything."

"Ah!" she said, with a little cry of disappointment, "my man said not to make too sure, and that the ways of the gentlefolks is hard to know."

"I cannot explain to you," I said, as gently as I could, "what it is that has made me forget you. It was an event that can only do you good in the end. Go home now, and see the man that took your things from you, and tell him to come to me. I promise you it shall all be put right."

The woman looked at me in astonishment, then burst forth, as it seemed, involuntarily, "What! without asking no questions?" After this there came a storm of tears and blessings, from which I made haste to escape, but not without carrying that curious commentary on my rashness away with me,—"Without asking no questions?" It might be foolish, perhaps; but after all, how slight a matter. To make the poor creature comfortable at the cost of what,—a box or two of cigars, perhaps, or some other trifle. And if it should be her own fault, or her husband's—what then? Had I been punished for all my faults, where should I have been now? And if the advantage should be only temporary, what then? To be relieved and comforted even for a day or two, was not that something to count in life? Thus I quenched the fiery dart of criticism which my protégée herself had thrown into the transaction, not without a certain sense of the humor of it. Its effect, however, was to make me less anxious to see my father, to repeat my proposal to him, and to call his attention to the cruelty performed in his name. This one case I had taken out of the category of wrongs to be righted, by assuming arbitrarily the position of Providence in my own person,—for, of course, I had bound myself to pay the poor creature's rent as well as redeem her goods,—and, whatever might happen to her in the future, had taken the past into my own hands. The man came presently to see me, who, it seems, had acted as my father's agent in the matter. "I don't know, sir, how Mr. Canning will take it," he said. "He don't want none of those irregular, bad-paying ones in his property. He always says as to look over it and let the rent run on is making things worse in the end. His rule is, 'Never more than a month, Stevens;' that's what Mr. Canning says to me, sir. He says, 'More than that they can't pay. It's no use trying.' And it's a good rule; it's a very good rule. He won't hear none of their stories, sir. Bless you, you'd never get a penny of rent from them small houses if you listened to their tales. But if so be as you'll pay Mrs. Jordan's rent, it's none of my business how it's paid, so long as it's paid, and I'll send her back her things. But they'll just have to be took next time," he added composedly. "Over and over; it's always the same story with them sort of poor folks,—they're too poor for anything, that's the truth," the man said.

Morphew came back to my room after my visitor was gone. "Mr. Philip," he said, "you'll excuse me, sir, but if you're going to pay all the poor folks' rent as have distresses put in, you may just go into the court at once, for it's without end—"

"I am going to be the agent myself, Morphew, and manage for my father; and we'll soon put a stop to that," I said, more cheerfully than I felt.

"Manage for—master," he said, with a face of consternation. "You, Mr. Philip!"

"You seem to have a great contempt for me, Morphew."

He did not deny the fact. He said with excitement, "Master, sir,—master don't let himself be put a stop to by any man. Master's—not one to be managed. Don't you quarrel with master, Mr. Philip, for the love of God." The old man was quite pale.

"Quarrel!" I said. "I have never quarrelled with my father, and I don't mean to begin now."

Morphew dispelled his own excitement by making up the fire, which was dying in the grate. It was a very mild spring evening, and he made up a great blaze which would have suited December. This is one of many ways in which an old servant will relieve his mind. He muttered all the time as he threw on the coals and wood. "He'll not like it,—we all know as he'll not like it. Master won't stand no meddling, Mr. Philip,"—this last he discharged at me like a flying arrow as he closed the door.

I soon found there was truth in what he said. My father was not angry, he was even half amused. "I don't think that plan of yours will hold water, Phil. I hear you have been paying rents and redeeming furniture,—that's an expensive game, and a very profitless one. Of course, so long as you are a benevolent gentleman acting for your own pleasure, it makes no difference to me. I am quite content if I get my money, even out of your pockets,—so long as it amuses you. But as my collector, you know, which you are good enough to propose to be—"

"Of course I should act under your orders," I said; "but at least you might be sure that I would not commit you to any—to any—" I paused for a word.

"Act of oppression," he said, with a smile—"piece of cruelty, exaction—there are half-a-dozen words—"

"Sir—" I cried.

"Stop, Phil, and let us understand each other. I hope I have always been a just man. I do my duty on my side, and I expect it from others. It is your benevolence that is cruel. I have calculated anxiously how much credit it is safe to allow; but I will allow no man, or woman either, to go beyond what he or she can make up. My law is fixed. Now you understand. My agents, as you call them, originate nothing; they execute only what I decide—"

"But then no circumstances are taken into account,—no bad luck, no evil chances, no loss unexpected."

"There are no evil chances," he said; "there is no bad luck; they reap as they sow. No, I don't go among them to be cheated by their stories, and spend quite unnecessary emotion in sympathizing with them. You will find it much better for you that I don't. I deal with them on a general rule, made, I assure you, not without a great deal of thought."

"And must it always be so?" I said. "Is there no way of ameliorating or bringing in a better state of things?"

"It seems not," he said; "we don't get 'no forrarder' in that direction so far as I can see." And then he turned the conversation to general matters.

I retired to my room greatly discouraged that night. In former ages—or so one is led to suppose—and in the lower primitive classes who still linger near the primeval type, action of any kind was, and is, easier than amid the complication of our higher civilization. A bad man is a distinct entity, against whom you know more or less what steps to take. A tyrant, an oppressor, a bad landlord, a man who lets miserable tenements at a rack-rent (to come down to particulars), and exposes his wretched tenants to all those abominations of which we have heard so much—well! he is more or less a satisfactory opponent. There he is, and there is nothing to be said for him—down with him! and let there be an end of his wickedness. But when, on the contrary, you have before you a good man, a just man, who has considered deeply a question which you allow to be full of difficulty; who regrets, but cannot, being human, avert the miseries which to some unhappy individuals follow from the very wisdom of his rule,—what can you do? What is to be done? Individual benevolence at haphazard may balk him here and there, but what have you to put in the place of his well-considered scheme? Charity which makes paupers? or what else? I had not considered the question deeply, but it seemed to me that I now came to a blank wall, which my vague human sentiment of pity and scorn could find no way to breach. There must be wrong somewhere, but where? There must be some change for the better to be made, but how?

I was seated with a book before me on the table, with my head supported on my hands. My eyes were on the printed page, but I was not reading; my mind was full of these thoughts, my heart of great discouragement and despondency,—a sense that I could do nothing, yet that there surely must and ought, if I but knew it, be something to do. The fire which Morphew had built up before dinner was dying out, the shaded lamp on my table left all the corners in a mysterious twilight. The house was perfectly still, no one moving: my father in the library, where, after the habit of many solitary years, he liked to be left alone, and I here in my retreat, preparing for the formation of similar habits. I thought all at once of the third member of the party, the new-comer, alone too in the room that had been hers; and there suddenly occurred to me a strong desire to take up my lamp and go to the drawing-room and visit her, to see whether her soft, angelic face would give any inspiration. I restrained, however, this futile impulse,—for what could the picture say?—and instead wondered what might have been had she lived, had she been there, warmly enthroned beside the warm domestic centre, the hearth which would have been a common sanctuary, the true home. In that case what might have been? Alas! the question was no more simple to answer than the other: she might have been there alone too, her husband's business, her son's thoughts, as far from her as now, when her silent representative held her old place in the silence and darkness. I had known it so, often enough. Love itself does not always give comprehension and sympathy. It might be that she was more to us there, in the sweet image of her undeveloped beauty, than she might have been had she lived and grown to maturity and fading, like the rest.

I cannot be certain whether my mind was still lingering on this not very cheerful reflection, or if it had been left behind, when the strange occurrence came of which I have now to tell. Can I call it an occurrence? My eyes were on my book, when I thought

I heard the sound of a door opening and shutting, but so far away and faint that if real at all it must have been in a far corner of the house. I did not move except to lift my eyes from the book as one does instinctively the better to listen; when—But I cannot tell, nor have I ever been able to describe exactly what it was. My heart made all at once a sudden leap in my breast. I am aware that this language is figurative, and that the heart cannot leap; but it is a figure so entirely justified by sensation, that no one will have any difficulty in understanding what I mean. My heart leaped up and began beating wildly in my throat, in my ears, as if my whole being had received a sudden and intolerable shock. The sound went through my head like the dizzy sound of some strange mechanism, a thousand wheels and springs circling, echoing, working in my brain. I felt the blood bound in my veins, my mouth became dry, my eyes hot; a sense of something insupportable took possession of me. I sprang to my feet, and then I sat down again. I cast a quick glance round me beyond the brief circle of the lamplight, but there was nothing there to account in any way for this sudden extraordinary rush of sensation, nor could I feel any meaning in it, any suggestion, any moral impression. I thought I must be going to be ill, and got out my watch and felt my pulse: it was beating furiously, about one hundred and twenty-five throbs in a minute. I knew of no illness that could come on like this without warning, in a moment, and I tried to subdue myself, to say to myself that it was nothing, some flutter of the nerves, some physical disturbance. I laid myself down upon my sofa to try if rest would help me, and kept still, as long as the thumping and throbbing of this wild, excited mechanism within, like a wild beast plunging and struggling, would let me. I am quite aware of the confusion of the metaphor; the reality was just so. It was like a mechanism deranged, going wildly with ever-increasing precipitation, like those horrible wheels that from time to time catch a helpless human being in them and tear him to pieces; but at the same time it was like a maddened living creature making the wildest efforts to get free.

When I could bear this no longer I got up and walked about my room; then having still a certain command of myself, though I could not master the commotion within me, I deliberately took down an exciting book from the shelf, a book of breathless adventure which had always interested me, and tried with that to break the spell. After a few minutes, however, I flung the book aside; I was gradually losing all power over myself. What I should be moved to do,—to shout aloud, to struggle with I know not what; or if I was going mad altogether, and next moment must be a raving lunatic,—I could not tell. I kept looking round, expecting I don't know what; several times with the corner of my eye I seemed to see a movement, as if some one was stealing out of sight; but when I looked straight, there was never anything but the plain outlines of the wall and carpet, the chairs standing in good order. At last I snatched up the lamp in my hand, and went out of the room. To look at the picture, which had been faintly showing in my imagination from time to time, the eyes, more anxious than ever, looking at me from out the silent air? But no; I passed the door of that room swiftly, moving, it seemed, without any volition of my own, and before I knew where I was going, went into my father's library with my lamp in my hand.

He was still sitting there at his writing-table; he looked up astonished to see me hurrying in with my light. "Phil!" he said, surprised. I remember that I shut the door behind me, and came up to him, and set down the lamp on his table. My sudden appearance alarmed him. "What is the matter?" he cried. "Philip, what have you been doing with yourself?"

I sat down on the nearest chair and gasped, gazing at him. The wild commotion ceased; the blood subsided into its natural channels; my heart resumed its place. I use such words as mortal weakness can to express the sensations I felt. I came to myself thus, gazing at him, confounded, at once by the extraordinary passion which I had gone through, and its sudden cessation. "The matter?" I cried; "I don't know what is the matter."

My father had pushed his spectacles up from his eyes. He appeared to me as faces appear in a fever, all glorified with light which is not in them,—his eyes glowing, his white hair shining like silver; but his looks were severe. "You are not a boy, that I should reprove you; but you ought to know better," he said.

Then I explained to him, so far as I was able, what had happened. Had happened? Nothing had happened. He did not understand me; nor did I, now that it was over, understand myself; but he saw enough to make him aware that the disturbance in me was serious, and not caused by any folly of my own. He was very kind as soon as he had assured himself of this, and talked, taking pains to bring me back to unexciting subjects. He had a letter in his hand with a very deep border of black when I came in. I observed it, without taking any notice or associating it with anything I knew. He had many correspondents; and although we were excellent friends, we had never been on those confidential terms which warrant one man in asking another from whom a special letter has come. We were not so near to each other as this, though we were father and son. After a while I went back to my own room, and finished the evening in my usual way, without any return of the excitement which, now that it was over, looked to me like some extraordinary dream. What had it meant? Had it meant anything? I said to myself that it must be purely physical, something gone temporarily amiss, which had righted itself. It was physical; the excitement did not affect my mind. I was independent of it all the time, a spectator of my own agitation, a clear proof that, whatever it was, it had affected my bodily organization alone.

Next day I returned to the problem which I had not been able to solve. I found out my petitioner in the back street, and that she was happy in the recovery of her possessions, which to my eyes indeed did not seem very worthy either of lamentation or delight. Nor was her house the tidy house which injured virtue should have when restored to its humble rights. She was not injured virtue, it was clear. She made me a great many curtseys, and poured forth a number of blessings. Her "man" came in while I was there, and hoped in a gruff voice that God would reward me, and that the old gentleman'd let 'em alone. I did not like the look of the man. It seemed to me that in the dark lane behind the house of a winter's night he would not be a pleasant person to find in one's way. Nor was this all: when I went out into the little street which it appeared was all, or almost all, my father's property, a number of groups formed in my way, and at least half-a-dozen applicants sidled up. "I've more claims nor

Mary Jordan any day," said one; "I've lived on Squire Canning's property, one place and another, this twenty year." "And what do you say to me?" said another; "I've six children to her two, bless you, sir, and ne'er a father to do for them." I believed in my father's rule before I got out of the street, and approved his wisdom in keeping himself free from personal contact with his tenants. Yet when I looked back upon the swarming thoroughfare, the mean little houses, the women at their doors all so open-mouthed and eager to contend for my favor, my heart sank within me at the thought that out of their misery some portion of our wealth came, I don't care how small a portion; that I, young and strong, should be kept idle and in luxury, in some part through the money screwed out of their necessities, obtained sometimes by the sacrifice of everything they prized! Of course I know all the ordinary commonplaces of life as well as any one,—that if you build a house with your hand or your money, and let it, the rent of it is your just due; and must be paid. But yet—

"Don't you think, sir," I said that evening at dinner, the subject being reintroduced by my father himself, "that we have some duty towards them when we draw so much from them?"

"Certainly," he said; "I take as much trouble about their drains as I do about my own."

"That is always something, I suppose."

"Something! it is a great deal; it is more than they get anywhere else. I keep them clean, as far as that's possible. I give them at least the means of keeping clean, and thus check disease, and prolong life, which is more, I assure you, than they've any right to expect."

I was not prepared with arguments as I ought to have been. That is all in the Gospel according to Adam Smith, which my father had been brought up in, but of which the tenets had begun to be less binding in my day. I wanted something more, or else something less; but my views were not so clear, nor my system so logical and well-built, as that upon which my father rested his conscience, and drew his percentage with a light heart.

Yet I thought there were signs in him of some perturbation. I met him one morning coming out of the room in which the portrait hung, as if he had gone to look at it stealthily. He was shaking his head, and saying "No, no," to himself, not perceiving me, and I stepped aside when I saw him so absorbed. For myself, I entered that room but little. I went outside, as I had so often done when I was a child, and looked through the windows into the still and now sacred place, which had always impressed me with a certain awe. Looked at so, the slight figure in its white dress seemed to be stepping down into the room from some slight visionary altitude, looking with that which had seemed to me at first anxiety, which I sometimes represented to myself now as a wistful curiosity, as if she were looking for the life which might have been hers. Where was the existence that had belonged to her, the sweet household place, the infant she had left? She would no more recognize the man who thus came to look at her as through a veil, with a mystic reverence, than I could recognize her. I could never be her child to her, any more than she could be a mother to me.

Thus time passed on for several quiet days. There was nothing to make us give any special heed to the passage of time, life being very uneventful and its habits unvaried. My mind was very much preoccupied by my father's tenants. He had a great deal of property in the town which was so near us,—streets of small houses, the best-paying property (I was assured) of any. I was very anxious to come to some settled conclusion: on the one hand, not to let myself be carried away by sentiment; on the other, not to allow my strongly roused feelings to fall into the blank of routine, as his had done. I was seated one evening in my own sitting-room, busy with this matter,—busy with calculations as to cost and profit, with an anxious desire to convince him, either that his profits were greater than justice allowed, or that they carried with them a more urgent duty than he had conceived.

It was night, but not late, not more than ten o'clock, the household still astir. Everything was quiet,—not the solemnity of midnight silence, in which there is always something of mystery, but the soft-breathing quiet of the evening, full of the faint habitual sounds of a human dwelling, a consciousness of life about. And I was very busy with my figures, interested, feeling no room in my mind for any other thought. The singular experience which had startled me so much had passed over very quickly, and there had been no return. I had ceased to think of it; indeed, I had never thought of it save for the moment, setting it down after it was over to a physical cause without much difficulty. At this time I was far too busy to have thoughts to spare for anything, or room for imagination; and when suddenly in a moment, without any warning, the first symptom returned, I started with it into determined resistance, resolute not to be fooled by any mock influence which could resolve itself into the action of nerves or ganglions. The first symptom; as before, was that my heart sprang up with a bound, as if a cannon had been fired at my ear. My whole being responded with a start. The pen fell out of my fingers, the figures went out of my head as if all faculty had departed; and yet I was conscious for a time at least of keeping my self-control. I was like the rider of a frightened horse, rendered almost wild by something which in the mystery of its voiceless being it has seen, something on the road which it will not pass, but wildly plunging, resisting every persuasion, turns from, with ever-increasing passion. The rider himself after a time becomes infected with this inexplainable desperation of terror, and I suppose I must have done so; but for a time I kept the upper hand. I would not allow myself to spring up as I wished, as my impulse was, but sat there doggedly, clinging to my books, to my table, fixing myself on I did not mind what, to resist the flood of sensation, of emotion, which was sweeping through me, carrying me away. I tried to continue my calculations. I tried to stir myself up with recollections of the miserable sights I had seen, the poverty, the helplessness. I tried to work myself into indignation; but all through these efforts I felt the contagion growing upon me, my mind falling into sympathy with all those straining faculties of the body, startled, excited, driven wild by something, I knew not what. It was not fear. I was like a ship at sea straining and plunging against wind and tide, but I was not afraid. I am obliged to use these metaphors, otherwise I could give no explanation of my condition, seized upon against my will, and torn from all those moorings of reason to which I clung with desperation, as long as I had the strength.

When I got up from my chair at last, the battle was lost, so far as my powers of self-control were concerned. I got up, or rather was dragged up, from my seat, clutching at these material things round me as with a last effort to hold my own. But that was no longer possible; I was overcome. I stood for a moment looking round me feebly, feeling myself begin to babble with stammering lips, which was the alternative of shrieking, and which I seemed to choose as a lesser evil. What I said was, "What am I to do?" and after a while, "What do you want me to do?" although throughout I saw no one, heard no voice, and had in reality not power enough in my dizzy and confused brain to know what I myself meant. I stood thus for a moment, looking blankly round me for guidance, repeating the question, which seemed after a time to become almost mechanical, "What do you want me to do?" though I neither knew to whom I addressed it nor why I said it. Presently—whether in answer, whether in mere yielding of nature, I cannot tell—I became aware of a difference: not a lessening of the agitation, but a softening, as if my powers of resistance being exhausted, a gentler force, a more benignant influence, had room. I felt myself consent to whatever it was. My heart melted in the midst of the tumult; I seemed to give myself up, and move as if drawn by some one whose arm was in mine, as if softly swept along, not forcibly, but with an utter consent of all my faculties to do I knew not what, for love of I knew not whom. For love,—that was how it seemed,—not by force, as when I went before. But my steps took the same course: I went through the dim passages in an exaltation indescribable, and opened the door of my father's room.

He was seated there at his table as usual, the light of the lamp falling on his white hair; he looked up with some surprise at the sound of the opening door. "Phil," he said, and with a look of wondering apprehension on his face, watched my approach. I went straight up to him and put my hand on his shoulder. "Phil, what is the matter? What do you want with me? What is it?" he said.

"Father, I can't tell you. I come not of myself. There must be something in it, though I don't know what it is. This is the second time I have been brought to you here."

"Are you going—?" He stopped himself. The exclamation had been begun with an angry intention. He stopped, looking at me with a scared look, as if perhaps it might be true.

"Do you mean mad? I don't think so. I have no delusions that I know of. Father, think—do you know any reason why I am brought here? for some cause there must be."

I stood with my hand upon the back of his chair. His table was covered with papers, among which were several letters with the broad black border which I had before observed. I noticed this now in my excitement without any distinct association of thoughts, for that I was not capable of; but the black border caught my eye. And I was conscious that he too gave a hurried glance at them, and with one hand swept them away.

"Philip," he said, pushing back his chair, "you must be ill, my poor boy. Evidently we have not been treating you rightly; you have been more ill all through than I supposed. Let me persuade you to go to bed."

"I am perfectly well," I said. "Father, don't let us deceive one another. I am neither a man to go mad nor to see ghosts. What it is that has got the command over me I can't tell; but there is some cause for it. You are doing something or planning something with which I have a right to interfere."

He turned round squarely in his chair, with a spark in his blue eyes. He was not a man to be meddled with. "I have yet to learn what can give my son a right to interfere. I am in possession of all my faculties, I hope."

"Father," I cried, "won't you listen to me? No one can say I have been undutiful or disrespectful. I am a man, with a right to speak my mind, and I have done so; but this is different. I am not here by my own will. Something that is stronger than I has brought me. There is something in your mind which disturbs—others. I don't know what I am saying. This is not what I meant to say; but you know the meaning better than I. Some one—who can speak to you only by me—speaks to you by me; and I know that you understand."

He gazed up at me, growing pale, and his underlip fell. I, for my part, felt that my message was delivered. My heart sank into a stillness so sudden that it made me faint. The light swam in my eyes; everything went round with me. I kept upright only by my hold upon the chair; and in the sense of utter weakness that followed, I dropped on my knees I think first, then on the nearest seat that presented itself, and, covering my face with my hands, had hard ado not to sob, in the sudden removal of that strange influence,—the relaxation of the strain.

There was silence between us for some time; then he said, but with a voice slightly broken, "I don't understand you, Phil. You must have taken some fancy into your mind which my slower intelligence—Speak out what you want to say. What do you find fault with? Is it all—all that woman Jordan?"

He gave a short, forced laugh as he broke off, and shook me almost roughly by the shoulder, saying, "Speak out! what—what do you want to say?"

"It seems, sir, that I have said everything." My voice trembled more than his, but not in the same way. "I have told you that I did not come by my own will,—quite otherwise. I resisted as long as I could: now all is said. It is for you to judge whether it was worth the trouble or not."

He got up from his seat in a hurried way. "You would have me as—mad as yourself," he said, then sat down again as quickly. "Come, Phil: if it will please you, not to make a breach,—the first breach between us,—you shall have your way. I consent to your looking into that matter about the poor tenants. Your mind shall not be upset about that, even though I don't enter into all your views."

"Thank you," I said; "but, father, that is not what it is."

"Then it is a piece of folly," he said angrily. "I suppose you mean—but this is a matter in which I choose to judge for myself."

"You know what I mean," I said, as quietly as I could, "though I don't myself know; that proves there is good reason for it. Will you do one thing for me before I leave you? Come with me into the drawing-room—"

"What end," he said, with again the tremble in his voice, "is to be served by that?"

"I don't very well know; but to look at her, you and I together, will always do something for us, sir. As for breach, there can be no breach when we stand there."

He got up, trembling like an old man, which he was, but which he never looked like save at moments of emotion like this, and told me to take the light; then stopped when he had got half-way across the room. "This is a piece of theatrical sentimentality," he said. "No, Phil, I will not go. I will not bring her into any such— Put down the lamp, and, if you will take my advice, go to bed."

"At least," I said, "I will trouble you no more, father, to-night. So long as you understand, there need be no more to say."

He gave me a very curt "good-night," and turned back to his papers,—the letters with the black edge, either by my imagination or in reality, always keeping uppermost. I went to my own room for my lamp, and then alone proceeded to the silent shrine in which the portrait hung. I at least would look at her to-night. I don't know whether I asked myself, in so many words, if it were she who—or if it was any one—I knew nothing; but my heart was drawn with a softness—born, perhaps, of the great weakness in which I was left after that visitation—to her, to look at her, to see, perhaps, if there was any sympathy, any approval in her face. I set down my lamp on the table where her little work-basket still was; the light threw a gleam upward upon her,—she seemed more than ever to be stepping into the room, coming down towards me, coming back to her life. Ah, no! her life was lost and vanished: all mine stood between her and the days she knew. She looked at me with eyes that did not change. The anxiety I had seen at first seemed now a wistful, subdued question; but that difference was not in her look but in mine.

I need not linger on the intervening time. The doctor who attended us usually, came in next day "by accident," and we had a long conversation. On the following day a very impressive yet genial gentleman from town lunched with us,—a friend of my father's, Dr. Something; but the introduction was hurried, and I did not catch his name. He, too, had a long talk with me afterwards, my father being called away to speak to some one on business. Dr.—— drew me out on the subject of the dwellings of the poor. He said he heard I took great interest in this question, which had come so much to the front at the present moment. He was interested in it too, and wanted to know the view I took. I explained at considerable length that my view did not concern the general subject, on which I had scarcely thought, so much as the individual mode of management of my father's estate. He was a most patient and intelligent listener, agreeing with me on some points, differing in others; and his visit was very pleasant. I had no idea until after of its special object; though a certain puzzled look and slight shake of the head when my father returned, might have thrown some light upon it. The report of the medical experts in my case must, however, have been quite satisfactory, for I heard nothing more of them. It was, I think, a fortnight later when the next and last of these strange experiences came.

This time it was morning, about noon,—a wet and rather dismal spring day. The half-spread leaves seemed to tap at the window, with an appeal to be taken in; the primroses, that showed golden upon the grass at the roots of the trees, just beyond the smooth-shorn grass of the lawn, were all drooped and sodden among their sheltering leaves. The very growth seemed dreary—the sense of spring in the air making the feeling of winter a grievance, instead of the natural effect which it had conveyed a few months before. I had been writing letters, and was cheerful enough, going back among the associates of my old life, with, perhaps, a little longing for its freedom and independence, but at the same time a not ungrateful consciousness that for the moment my present tranquillity might be best.

This was my condition—a not unpleasant one—when suddenly the now well-known symptoms of the visitation to which I had become subject suddenly seized upon me,—the leap of the heart; the sudden, causeless, overwhelming physical excitement, which I could neither ignore nor allay. I was terrified beyond description, beyond reason, when I became conscious that this was about to begin over again: what purpose did it answer; what good was in it? My father indeed understood the meaning of it though I did not understand; but it was little agreeable to be thus made a helpless instrument, without any will of mine, in an operation of which I knew nothing; and to enact the part of the oracle unwillingly, with suffering and such a strain as it took me days to get over. I resisted, not as before, but yet desperately, trying with better knowledge to keep down the growing passion. I hurried to my room and swallowed a dose of a sedative which had been given me to procure sleep on my first return from India. I saw Morphew in the hall, and called him to talk to him, and cheat myself, if possible, by that means. Morphew lingered, however, and, before he came, I was beyond conversation. I heard him speak, his voice coming vaguely through the turmoil which was already in my ears, but what he said I have never known. I stood staring, trying to recover my power of attention, with an aspect which ended by completely frightening the man. He cried out at last that he was sure I was ill, that he must bring me something; which words penetrated more or less into my maddened brain. It became impressed upon me that he was going to get some one—one of my father's doctors, perhaps—to prevent me from acting, to stop my interference, and that if I waited a moment longer I might be too late. A vague idea seized me at the same time, of taking refuge with the portrait,—going to its feet, throwing myself there, perhaps, till the paroxysm should be over. But it was not there that my footsteps were directed. I can remember making an effort to open the door of the drawing-room, and feeling myself swept past it, as if by a gale of wind. It was not there that I had to go. I knew very well where I had to go,—once more on my confused and voiceless mission to my father, who understood, although I could not understand.

Yet as it was daylight, and all was clear, I could not help noting one or two circumstances on my way. I saw some one sitting in the hall as if waiting,—a woman, a girl, a black-shrouded figure, with a thick veil over her face; and asked myself who she was, and what she wanted there. This question, which had nothing to do with my present condition, somehow got into my mind, and was tossed up and down upon the tumultuous tide like a stray log on the breast of a fiercely rolling stream, now submerged, now coming uppermost, at the mercy of the waters. It did not stop me for a moment, as I hurried towards my father's room, but it got upon the current of my mind. I flung open my father's door, and closed it again after me, without seeing who was there or how he was engaged. The full clearness of the daylight did not identify him as the lamp did at night. He looked up at the sound of the door, with a glance of apprehension; and rising suddenly, interrupting some one who was standing speaking to him with much earnestness and even vehemence, came forward to meet me. "I cannot be disturbed at present," he said quickly; "I am busy." Then seeing the look in my face, which by this time he knew, he too changed color. "Phil," he said, in a low, imperative voice, "wretched boy, go away—go away; don't let a stranger see you—"

"I can't go away," I said. "It is impossible. You know why I have come. I cannot, if I would. It is more powerful than I—"

"Go, sir," he said; "go at once; no more of this folly. I will not have you in this room: Go-go!"

I made no answer. I don't know that I could have done so. There had never been any struggle between us before; but I had no power to do one thing or another. The tumult within me was in full career. I heard indeed what he said, and was able to reply; but his words, too, were like straws tossed upon the tremendous stream. I saw now with my feverish eyes who the other person present was. It was a woman, dressed also in mourning similar to the one in the hall; but this a middle-aged woman, like a respectable servant. She had been crying, and in the pause caused by this encounter between my father and myself, dried her eyes with a handkerchief, which she rolled like a ball in her hand, evidently in strong emotion. She turned and looked at me as my father spoke to me, for a moment with a gleam of hope, then falling back into her former attitude.

My father returned to his seat. He was much agitated too, though doing all that was possible to conceal it. My inopportune arrival was evidently a great and unlooked-for vexation to him. He gave me the only look of passionate displeasure I have ever had from him, as he sat down again; but he said nothing more.

"You must understand," he said, addressing the woman, "that I have said my last words on this subject. I don't choose to enter into it again in the presence of my son, who is not well enough to be made a party to any discussion. I am sorry that you should have had so much trouble in vain, but you were warned beforehand, and you have only yourself to blame. I acknowledge no claim, and nothing you can say will change my resolution. I must beg you to go away. All this is very painful and quite useless. I acknowledge no claim."

"Oh, sir," she cried, her eyes beginning once more to flow, her speech interrupted by little sobs. "Maybe I did wrong to speak of a claim. I'm not educated to argue with a gentleman. Maybe we have no claim. But if it's not by right, oh, Mr. Canning, won't you let your heart be touched by pity? She don't know what I'm saying, poor dear. She's not one to beg and pray for herself, as I'm doing for her. Oh, sir, she's so young! She's so lone in this world,—not a friend to stand by her, nor a house to take her in! You are the nearest to her of any one that's left in this world. She hasn't a relation,—not one so near as you,—oh!" she cried, with a sudden thought, turning quickly round upon me, "this gentleman's your son! Now I think of it, it's not your relation she is, but his, through his mother! That's nearer, nearer! Oh, sir! you're young; your heart should be more tender. Here is my young lady that has no one in the world to look to her. Your own flesh and blood; your mother's cousin,—your mother's—"

My father called to her to stop, with a voice of thunder. "Philip, leave us at once. It is not a matter to be discussed with you."

And then in a moment it became clear to me what it was. It had been with difficulty that I had kept myself still. My breast was laboring with the fever of an impulse poured into me, more than I could contain. And now for the first time I knew why. I hurried towards him, and took his hand, though he resisted, into mine. Mine were burning, but his like ice: their touch burnt me with its chill, like fire. "This is what it is?" I cried. "I had no knowledge before. I don't know now what is being asked of you. But, father, understand! You know, and I know now, that some one sends me,—some one—who has a right to interfere."

He pushed me away with all his might. "You are mad," he cried. "What right have you to think—? Oh, you are mad—mad! I have seen it coming on—"

The woman, the petitioner, had grown silent, watching this brief conflict with the terror and interest with which women watch a struggle between men. She started and fell back when she heard what he said, but did not take her eyes off me, following every movement I made. When I turned to go away, a cry of indescribable disappointment and remonstrance burst from her, and even my father raised himself up and stared at my withdrawal, astonished to find that he had overcome me so soon and easily. I paused for a moment, and looked back on them, seeing them large and vague through the mist of fever. "I am not going away," I said. "I am going for another messenger,—one you can't gainsay."

My father rose. He called out to me threateningly, "I will have nothing touched that is hers. Nothing that is hers shall be profaned—"

I waited to hear no more; I knew what I had to do. By what means it was conveyed to me I cannot tell; but the certainty of an influence which no one thought of calmed me in the midst of my fever. I went out into the hall, where I had seen the young stranger waiting. I went up to her and touched her on the shoulder. She rose at once, with a little movement of alarm, yet with docile and instant obedience, as if she had expected the summons. I made her take off her veil and her bonnet, scarcely looking at her, scarcely seeing her, knowing how it was: I took her soft, small, cool, yet trembling hand into mine; it was so soft and cool,—not cold,—it refreshed me with its tremulous touch. All through I moved and spoke like a man in a dream; swiftly, noiselessly, all the complications of waking life removed; without embarrassment, without reflection, without the loss of a moment. My father was still standing up, leaning a little forward as he had done when I withdrew; threatening, yet terror-stricken, not knowing what I might be about to do, when I returned with my companion. That was the one thing he had not thought of. He was entirely undecided, unprepared. He gave her one look, flung up his arms above his head, and uttered a distracted cry, so wild that it seemed the last outcry of nature,—"Agnes!" then fell back like a sudden ruin, upon himself, into his chair.

I had no leisure to think how he was, or whether he could hear what I said. I had my message to deliver. "Father," I said, laboring with my panting breath, "it is for this that heaven has opened, and one whom I never saw, one whom I know not, has taken possession of me. Had we been less earthly, we should have seen her—herself, and not merely her image. I have not even known what she meant. I have been as a fool without understanding. This is the third time I have come to you with her message, without knowing what to say. But now I have found it out. This is her message. I have found it out at last." There was an awful pause,—a pause in which no one moved or breathed. Then there came a broken voice out of my father's chair. He had not understood, though I think he heard what I said. He put out two feeble hands. "Phil—I think I am dying—has she—has she come for me?" he said.

We had to carry him to his bed. What struggles he had gone through before I cannot tell. He had stood fast, and had refused to be moved, and now he fell,—like an old tower, like an old tree. The necessity there was for thinking of him saved me from the physical consequences which had prostrated me on a former occasion. I had no leisure now for any consciousness of how matters went with myself.

His delusion was not wonderful, but most natural. She was clothed in black from head to foot, instead of the white dress of the portrait. She had no knowledge of the conflict, of nothing but that she was called for, that her fate might depend on the next few minutes. In her eyes there was a pathetic question, a line of anxiety in the lids, an innocent appeal in the looks. And the face the same: the same lips, sensitive, ready to quiver; the same innocent, candid brow; the look of a common race, which is more subtle than mere resemblance. How I knew that it was so I cannot tell, nor any man. It was the other, the elder,—ah, no! not elder; the ever young, the Agnes to whom age can never come, she who they say was the mother of a man who never saw her,—it was she who led her kinswoman, her representative, into our hearts.

My father recovered after a few days: he had taken cold, it was said, the day before; and naturally, at seventy, a small matter is enough to upset the balance even of a strong man. He got quite well; but he was willing enough afterwards to leave the management of that ticklish kind of property which involves human well-being in my hands, who could move about more freely, and see with my own eyes how things were going on. He liked home better, and had more pleasure in his personal existence in the end of his life. Agnes is now my wife, as he had, of course, foreseen. It was not merely the disinclination to receive her father's daughter, or to take upon him a new responsibility, that had moved him, to do him justice; but both these motives had told strongly. I have never been told, and now will never be told, what his griefs against my mother's family, and specially against that cousin, had been; but that he had been very determined, deeply prejudiced, there can be no doubt. It turned out after, that the first occasion on which I had been mysteriously commissioned to him with a message which I did not understand, and which for that time he did not understand, was the evening of the day on which he had received the dead man's letter, appealing to him—to him, a man whom he had wronged—on behalf of the child who was about to be left friendless in the world. The second time, further letters—from the nurse who was the only guardian of the orphan, and the chaplain of the place where her father had died, taking it for granted that my father's house was her natural refuge—had been received. The third I have already described, and its results.

For a long time after, my mind was never without a lurking fear that the influence which had once taken possession of me might return again. Why should I have feared to be influenced, to be the messenger of a blessed creature, whose wishes could be nothing but heavenly? Who can say? Flesh and blood is not made for such encounters: they were more than I could bear. But nothing of the kind has ever occurred again.

Agnes had her peaceful domestic throne established under the picture. My father wished it to be so, and spent his evenings there in the warmth and light, instead of in the old library,—in the narrow circle cleared by our lamp out of the darkness, as long as he lived. It is supposed by strangers that the picture on the wall is that of my wife; and I have always been glad that it should be so supposed. She who was my mother, who came back to me and became as my soul for three strange moments and no more, but with whom I can feel no credible relationship as she stands there, has retired for me into the tender regions of the unseen. She has passed once more into the secret company of those shadows, who can only become real in an atmosphere fitted to modify and harmonize all differences, and make all wonders possible,—the light of the perfect day.

www.ingramcontent.com/pod-product-compliance
Lightning Source LLC
Chambersburg PA
CBHW011518170626
46810CB00009B/3402

* 9 7 8 1 6 3 6 3 7 4 3 7 6 *